Serendipity's Debt

By

C. A. King

Cover Design:

JUST WRITE CREATIONS

Editor:

Karen Hrdlicka

If you believe this book is dedicated to you,

perhaps it is!

Cover Design: **Just Write Creations**

First Printing: March 2019

ISBN: 978-1-988301-77-8

Kings Toe Publishing

kingstoepublishing@gmail.com

Brantford, Ontario. Canada

Welcome to Knollville

Whether it's the Windy City or the one that never sleeps, almost every place imaginable has its own specific claim to fame. Some, admittedly, are more peculiar than others. Let's face it, visiting the world's largest garden gnome is most likely not on everyone's bucket list. In other parts of the world, true wonders go unheard of. Only a select few travellers would find the petrifying lake in Tanzania worth visiting. A place where animals turn to statues when they die is the fodder true fear uses to spawn its finest nightmares.

Knollville, located in the heart of Knoll County, is no different... other than the fact it is best known for its almost total obscurity.

It's not marked on any map and there aren't any road signs along the way. Whether one believes it to be a supernatural hot spot or a naturally occurring magnetic field, a GPS isn't able to locate it. In fact, the lady barking instructions through the device tends to become a bit confused within a fifty-mile radius.

If a traveller does manage to stumble upon Knollville, they are in luck. The diverse scenery the city and surrounding area have to offer makes the trip worthwhile. Visitors can climb mountains, explore valleys, canoe down rivers and lakes, hike in vast forests, and each comes with its own folk lore. Be forewarned, though, not all of the tales the locals tell are for the faint of heart.

There is a fine line drawn between the boundaries of reality and the paranormal. These stories teeter on that line. Like the explanation for the failing GPS, there are arguments for both science and the unknown. Serendipity's Debt is one of those tales. Can it be explained, or is the supernatural at play? That is one question readers will have to answer for themselves.

Welcome to Knollville...

Previously in Knollville

(An excerpt from Truly Unfortunate)

Miranda rushed down the hall, a sense of urgency pulsing through her veins. She'd never been a true believer, but this case had her second-guessing the boundaries of reality. A part of her couldn't help but hope her partner received her call and hadn't done anything stupid. The odds were against her; Jeff never listened to his voicemail messages.

She hopped from foot to foot, waiting for the red light to turn green. Grasping the handle too soon, the lock refused to open. She started the process all over again, jumping around worse than a child in need of a bathroom. This time, she waited for the buzz followed by the lock grinding open before she pulled.

Her first sight was her partner sitting at the sterile table. A black and white pen rolled back and forth between his hands. His gaze never once faltered from its movements.

"Jeff," Miranda said, her voice squeaking. She cleared her throat with a hoarse cough. "Please tell me you didn't use that thing."

Jeff chuckled. "I don't need to write anything," he said, pushing the pen towards the middle of the table. He slouched back in the plastic chair.

"That's not what I meant," Miranda snapped.

"I know what you meant," Jeff answered, frowning. "In the end, I didn't have the nerve."

"Good," Miranda said, taking a seat across from her partner. "It might sound crazy, but after talking to the psychic, I think there might be more to Damionion than we might want to admit."

Jeff let out a huff. "Ya think?" he replied. "Doctor Stevenson is dead. It was an accident, of course. A fire took not only his life, but his life's work, too. A novelty fortune-telling ball survived. It was found rolling around the ashes. It's in the box."

"Truly?"

"Gone," Jeff said, sitting up. "The captain released her when all the evidence went up in smoke."

"Where does that leave us?" Miranda asked.

"With two boxes to carry to storage," Captain Miller replied from the door. "I'll walk with you." He motioned with his head for the detectives to follow. They caught up to him waiting for their ride down to arrive.

Whoever created the elevator didn't have comfort in mind. The tiny cubicle boasted a certificate stating over a dozen people could ride at once. After piling the three of them and two boxes in, they were no more than sardines jammed into a can. No one said it, but with little room to move, they were all secretly thanking their lucky stars their companions all showered and wore deodorant on a daily basis.

Jeff detached his security pass to swipe access to the files room.

"I got it," the captain said, removing a card from his pocket. He turned his back to the doors.

The lift's gears began to grind, halting the descent, but the doors remained closed.

"Other way," the captain whispered.

Jeff and Miranda exchanged glances before turning to face the back of the elevator. It opened to a dimly-lit corridor they had never seen before.

"I thought we were going to file these," Miranda stated. "The Knollville case files are kept in a room the other way."

"Yes," Captain Miller agreed, "but the Knollville curse files are kept through there."

"Knollville curses?!" Miranda shrieked, quickening her pace to catch up to her partner who was already leaps and bounds ahead.

A set of double doors, which belonged in a hospital rather than a police department, stood between Jeff and the understanding he needed. He pushed hard, sending them swinging open. Inside was a complete duplicate of the department above them, lacking only officers at each of the desks.

"You made it, I see!" Henry Doogalen declared. "I was wondering if the captain's intuition about you two was a bit off."

"Can I ask..." Jeff started.

"This department handles unexplained files," the captain stated. "Most of the cases that end up down here require a certain willingness to take a few leaps of faith on the part of the investigators, in order to be solved."

"Are we talking paranormal or alien?" Jeff asked.

"Both," Henry answered, a grin peeking out from under his moustache. "Have you ever noticed that Knollville isn't on any map?"

"Not really," Jeff replied, shrugging his shoulders. "Most people have a GPS nowadays."

"How ancient I've become," Henry chuckled. "Let me rephrase that... have you noticed if you leave Knollville and use your GPS to return, the woman calling out directions at you becomes a bit confused? She might tell you to take a U-turn a few hundred times on the same road or ask you to veer to the left, landing you in a lake."

"No," Jeff admitted. "If I leave here, I pretty much know how to get back. I don't use a GPS."

"Okay," Henry said. "If you did, you would have noticed. Knollville is the hardest place in existence to find when you don't know where it is."

"What does this have to do with anything?" Miranda asked. "We patrol what happens in Knollville."

"Because of its secluded nature, Knollville attracts some unusual individuals," Henry replied. "You can read up on some of the recent cases if you want. Bottom line, we live in a paranormal hotspot. This department polices that side of things."

"What does that have to do with us?" Jeff asked.

"Henry is retiring," the captain announced. "He's well past the age and is lacing up the boots. All we've been waiting for is the right duo to come along to fill them. I would like the two of you to take a hold of the reins."

"You want us to become ghost hunters?" Miranda questioned, her nose crinkling up.

Henry chuckled. "In a sense, yes," he replied. "It's a whole lot more, too. You witnessed yourself how normal residents can become tangled in the affairs of the supernatural. You two would be ensuring their safety."

"We couldn't save anyone this time," Jeff scoffed. "What makes you think we can serve and protect against a herd of zombies?"

"I've worked this department for fifteen years and I don't have that answer," Henry admitted. "I do know we, as officers, have a duty to do our best to keep good people safe. No one is asking any more than that."

"Fifteen years?" One of Jeff's eyebrows arched as he glanced at the older officer. "That was when..."

"When I met Truly," Henry replied. "Yes. That case has haunted me my whole career. I imagine it will do the same to you. Even in this department, in most of the files, the loose ends tie together creating a satisfactory ending... a hard to believe one, but it's closure nonetheless. When it comes to Truly, we may never know if those deaths belonged in this department, were accidents or should have been treated as unsolved murders."

"So a part of you does believe the girl could have been to blame," Jeff stated.

"As I said before, *could have* is a broad term," Henry explained. "The thought was always there that Geena might have been the only accidental death. I'll always have questions. Was there a man? If yes, was he of a supernatural descent? If no, was Truly behind it all?" He sighed.

"Who else would we be working with?" Jeff questioned.

"You would report to me," the captain stated. "No one else needs to know about your work. You have the full resources of the department at your fingertips at all times. The positions come with a pay increase as well."

Miranda shrugged her shoulders. "I'm in," she blurted out. "When do we start?"

Jeff darted a glance in her direction.

"What?!" she asked. "I enjoyed checking out the psychic shop. There's a whole world out there you and I chose to ignore. I, for one, am opening my eyes." She snapped her fingers.

"I guess you have two new paranormal detectives," Jeff said, rubbing his hands together. "Where do we start?"

Chapter One

Some days, the frosting on the last piece of carrot cake was doubled and the barista spelt her name correctly on the coffee cup. This wasn't one of those. This was the day the alarm clock broke and there wasn't even a minute to spare to stop for a coffee.

Her mama always called it, *Life's way of bringing balance to the universe*. Seren, as much as she loved her mother, disagreed. She wasn't the type of person who looked for the good in everything that happened. The grass was always greener and not only on the other side. It was better everywhere other than under her own feet. There was nothing wrong with wanting more and reaching out to grab it.

The thing to keep in mind when faced with having the worst day of one's life, was another tended to be lurking around the corner somewhere, waiting for an opportunity to pounce. Those were the exact moments the fates, out of the blue, decided to compete with one another to see which could best mess up a poor soul's life in the most hideous of ways.

The three had finally achieved perfection; taking a cake, eating it, and spitting it back up all over her. There had always been not-so-perfect days. Those were easy to handle. That particular day, however, a new level of torture was added into the mix and it was specifically made just for her.

Seren threw her arms up in the air at yet another bus speeding by, without so much as even hitting the brakes. Every second that passed inched her farther away from any chance at a big promotion. That position had her name all over it. The only problem was, no one else seemed to agree. Still, she tossed her resume into the application pile, crossing her fingers and toes someone would take notice.

The company was ready to announce a winner any day. This was the biggest lottery of her life, and she sank her life's savings into buying as many tickets as she could. If it didn't end with a raise and corner office, things were bound to go in the opposite direction. She wanted to stand on equal footing with management not in the unemployment line.

Seren hobbled along, wishing she hadn't worn shiny new shoes meant to impress. Six-inch heels weren't meant for climbing ladders, even if they were corporate ones. A blister was already forming, growing bigger with every rub of her foot and that amounted to every step. Once it fully formed, she'd be in trouble and not just from the pain. If it popped, there'd be a mess to clean up. No one wanted to see that, or hear her whine about it.

A bus crawled by in a slow motion taunt; a blatant mock that served its purpose. Her last nerve stood on edge, waiting for the opportune chance to explode. The next stop was in her sights, but still a distance away. The race was on to see who would make it there first. Of course, she never actually had a chance. No ordinary person could out-run a bus. Still, she picked up the pace, hopping on the spot just long enough to pull off her shoes. The black heels waved furiously in the air, to no avail.

The driver didn't so much as flinch as the doors closed, leaving her gagging on the sidewalk with a mouthful of exhaust. Someone needed to write a letter to the mayor about city buses being made a smidgen more environmentally friendly. She, of course, wasn't that person. There'd be a P.T.A. soccer mom, with overachiever written across her forehead, who would handle that.

Seren bent over at the waist, hoping that trying to catch her breath would prove easier than catching a ride with the Knollville public transportation system. Her toes wiggled back at her, having broken free from their stockings.

"Great!"

The nylon leggings had been as new as the shoes that morning. They hadn't lasted longer than two blocks. Between the holes in the front and blood stains forming in the back, they were soon-to-be part of the next garbage pickup. Unfortunately, she couldn't scrap them in public. Even if she could, there was another problem to deal with. She couldn't remember the last time she shaved her legs. Colder weather meant they were usually covered up and she forwent the ritual.

There were those women who claimed hair, no matter where on the body, was empowering, and perhaps it was. Their agenda wasn't something worth worrying about. Being an activist was fine and dandy when it was someone else making the waves. For those barely squeaking by in life, taking a stand was a mistake. The bottom line was, those higher up in the chain of command at work weren't concerned with how being hairy made her feel. All that mattered to them was she showed up on time, sporting a tidy appearance. There had already been enough flack aimed in her direction over her continually frizzy hair.

Seren glanced up at the sky. "Please let something go right for me," she begged.

Chapter Two

Seren fell back into her chair with a sigh of relief. The worst commute in history was in the books. Whoever said public transportation was the better choice, hadn't gone through the ordeal she just had. Buying a car was looking better by the minute. Of course, she needed the promotion, and the pay raise that came along with it, to be able to afford one. That was a never-ending cycle; the car was needed to get the job, the job was needed to get the car. She ended up with neither.

"You're late!" Ms. Parker exclaimed, her eyes glaring down over silver-brimmed, round glasses, forming the most condescending stare humanly possible. "We've been waiting for your reports all morning." The frown lines on her face enlarged, the crevices screaming for a new injection of Botox.

Seren opened her mouth to speak, but was met with a hand held palm forward in front of her face. Any closer and it would have entered the personal bubble human resources always lectured about. She bit her tongue, awaiting the verbal lashing her superior expected her to sit back and take.

"I don't want to hear your excuses. The meeting adjourned five minutes ago," Ms. Parker complained. "You've wasted the time of everyone on the board. Make sure the report is on Mr. Burns's desk before you leave today. He will be looking it over tomorrow morning first thing, and I won't take the chance of you not being here on time again. Are we clear?"

Seren nodded her head, her hands shaking beneath the cover of her desk. This wasn't the first time she'd messed up and, knowing her, it wasn't going to be the last, either. How could she have faith in herself if no one else had any in her?

Ms. Parker stomped away, surrounded by a cloud of disappointment, which no doubt, would end up raining on several employees' parades throughout the day.

Seren let out huff, the air blowing a stray curl off her face. It bounced back in defiance. Not even curls listened to her. Something had to change. If she was going to move up in the company, she needed to take a page out of Ms. Parker's playbook. What the woman lacked in feminine appeal, she made up for in tidiness. Every hair on her head was in place, pulled back into a perfect bun. Even they were afraid of falling victim to her wraith.

Seren fumbled for her purse, one hand disappearing into the depths of the unknown. It felt its way around the bottom, pushing loose change and bits of garbage aside. Not finding the treasure she sought, the bag shook, moving things around. Frown lines deepened, as her tongue darted out the corner of her mouth.

There was no rhyme or reason to the blind approach. Looking inside, probably would have saved time and effort. Logic never seemed to be on Seren's side. Neither was patience. The purse tipped upside down, its contents spilling all over her desk and floor. Glares co-workers were tossing her way were the least of her concerns. Finding the flash drive her superiors wanted was all that mattered.

Fatherly advice sounded in her head. "If at first you can't see the answer you are looking for, eliminate that which isn't a part of the equation." He might not have been referring to her purse, but he still hit the nail on the head. He always did.

Picking out the bits of paper, old receipts, and even older mints, she tossed them in the garbage. Pens, paperclips, and other office supplies went straight into an upper drawer. That left a handful of change, a small shadow box that belonged to her parents, a hairbrush, a wallet, a single bandage and a couple of tampons.

Two fingers tapped on her temple. She needed to retrace her steps. If she lost those files, she could pretty much kiss that promotion goodbye, not that she had much of a chance at it in the first place.

That morning had been a particularly bad one. When the alarm clock forgot to wake her, it threw everything else off kilter. Things went downhill from there, from the apartment building's hot water being used up before she jumped in, to the coffee maker spitting grounds out instead of liquid. Crunchy coffee wasn't a food group, or at least it shouldn't have been one.

All those things came to mind easily. What happened to the flash drive, however, eluded her. It had been attached to her computer. Of that, she was positive. She even vaguely remembered removing the stick, but not where it ended up; perhaps it was left on the table...

"Ms. Parker won't like seeing that mess," Molly suggested in no more than a whisper. Glancing over from a neighbouring desk, she offered a meek smile, before returning to her data entry.

Seren side-eyed her co-worker. That was probably the most anyone, other than Ms. Parker, had said to her in all the years she worked there.

Their department wasn't a glorious one. Workers sat at their desks, with only half partitions separating them. There wasn't a need for anything more. All they were expected to do was keep their heads down and their fingers moving, hitting strokes on their keyboards as they chipped away at whatever assignments they had been given. The job was as grey and dismal as the colour of the walls and carpets.

There was no point to socializing or drinks after work when, on any given day, the person next to you might not be the same as the day before. The employment turn over rate for the company was off the charts. People constantly applied to work there, though. The extra twenty-five cents an hour to start appealed to anyone in need of a job. That wasn't what mattered to Seren. It had been the promise of a chance for advancement in the ranks that had sealed the deal for her.

As disorganized as she was, she'd still managed to make it through five years of service, giving her seniority. Her bungling, apparently, wasn't as bad as those who broke into tears on their first meeting with Ms. Parker. Some simply never came back; others lasted a day or two. If a timid fool managed to stay an entire week, they'd find a pink slip waiting for them with their pay. Their company had no room for emotional weakness.

Seren returned to the mess at hand, sorting the remainder with some items falling back into her purse and the rest into a drawer. A huff of air escaped puffed out cheeks.

There wasn't enough time to go home and back during lunch. The best she could do was hope the stick was sitting, waiting for her -- then leave extra early in the morning to make sure the files ended up where they needed to be on time.

Worry was the bane of all existence. It did absolutely no good whatsoever, and yet, was completely unavoidable. Everyone did it. The stack of files in her inbox went down slower than usual, her mind wandering to the missing flash drive. If only she remembered where she put it. Then, maybe, she would be able to breathe easy again.

A hangnail shared her concern, finding its way between teeth. She chomped down, pulling the skin. A little too much force left it stinging. Her top drawer opened, in hopes a bandage stayed near the top. She riffled things around, before declaring success, just in time. Any longer and a drop of blood might have stained the white sheets of paper she was working on. It affixed easily around the newly-formed wound.

Seren reached for her last file, glancing at the clock at the same time. There were still a few hours in the work day left. As if on cue, Ms. Parker returned, dropping a stack of files in the empty tray.

"Make sure those are done before you leave this evening," she barked. "You should have come to pick them up hours ago." Her nose stuck in the air, sniffing out some other frightened soul to torment.

Seren sighed. Even if she was on top of her game, the new pile wasn't a job that could be completed in a couple of hours. She spent too much time brooding over yesterday's work and not enough on today's. Her head hung down with something else to worry about. The day was becoming longer by the minute.

Time was an unusual thing that she'd never fully understood. If she wanted to go somewhere, she could literally see the hands slowing down to torment her. If she had too much to do, however, it flew by unnoticed.

Co-workers were already happily shutting their stations down for the night, while she still had a fair number of tasks to complete. If there were a way to turn back time and start the day over, she gladly would have. That wasn't her superpower, though. She rubbed the back of her neck, determined to waste as little time as possible.

The final file had barely landed in her outbox before her purse was in hand. Having already missed breakfast and skipped lunch, being late for dinner meant she was ravenous.

The office door slammed behind her, locking. She didn't so much as glance back, in fear of more work jumping out at her before she managed to make a full escape. As it was, she was already in another race.

Her bus home was due to arrive anytime. There were only a few minutes left. Making it to the stop and not playing another round of peek-a-boo with public transit was the only thing on her mind.

Thunder crackled in the sky. A flash of lightning suggested a storm was imminent. She vaguely remembered hearing a weather report in the background before she leaving home.

Seren snapped her fingers, remembering exactly where the flash drive was... right beside the umbrella she had forgotten to bring. The first drops of rain teased a light shower. Within moments, though, the drops became pellets, pounding down with the force of hundreds of paint guns aimed point-blank at her exposed skin.

She doubled-checked her watch as her bus appeared in the distance. No public transportation was ever early. It was either on time or late. Those were the rules. This driver must have been new. He defied the unwritten laws of public transit. Even worse, his bus was the last one on the rush hour schedule. A complete hour would pass by before another one came by. Knowing her luck, that one would be late.

Her paced quickened, then came to an abrupt stop a few yards from the sign. One foot refused to move. Seren glanced down at the heel of her shoe wedged tightly in a crack in the sidewalk. She pulled harder, desperate to free herself, but only managing to topple over in the process. A crack as loud as thunder sounded at the same time the heel broke off.

Pushing her soaked hair aside, she stood on one foot, arms waving furiously at the driver; yelling for him to stop. Whether or not he saw her, she'd never know. A mouthful of dirty water was all she received for her efforts. Had it happened someone else, it might have been humorous. A girl standing in the rain, soaked with knees bloodied from a fall, and a broken shoe in one hand.

She groaned. That particular bus stop lacked a shelter to wait in. She weighed her choices; walk to the next stop or stand, allowing the rain to leave welts on her skin.

A city garbage can was the new proud owner of a brand new pair of broken shoes. One day was a new record for her. Usually, they lasted a month or two before she did something stupid. She wiggled her toes still exposed from the morning's fiasco. If she walked, there'd be a few more sores on her feet by the time she reached her apartment building. Sidewalks weren't designed for bare feet.

A car sped by. Water, which had pooled on the road, flew up, forming a tidal wave aimed directly in her path. She clenched her eyes and lips tightly, knowing what was coming. That was the final straw. She wasn't about to stand there a moment longer, forced to take the abuse of cruel drivers. They had a warm, dry seat, yet they doled out pedestrian punishments like a jury of her peers -- the judgement: guilty of witchcraft. The sentence had been chosen, a soaking through to the bones, using enough water to properly drown any normal human being. There was bound to be repercussions, too. If she wasn't sniffling and sneezing by the morning, it would be a miracle.

Two blocks was as far as she managed to trudge under the waterlogged weight of her clothes and hair. The rain was relentless, each drop longing to leave her skin that much more icy and pale than the last one. She rubbed her eyes furiously, wishing they came equipped with wipers. Barely making out a sign flashing the word *open*, she headed to a bar on the other side of the street.

The wind fought her every step, blowing her backward and whipping loose strands of hair against her face. The entrance was almost in reach. Every muscle tensed as she put all of her weight behind one final push. It took one foot on a wall and both hands on the handle to force the door to budge. Once it opened, there was a new problem to deal with. It wasn't about to close easily, at least not with her strength. She glanced over her shoulder. A sigh of relief escaped her lips, disappearing out the open door. A man was coming to her aid from behind the bar.

Chapter Three

"I'll have another," Mike said, waving an empty beer mug in the air at the bartender.

There was no sense being dry; nothing else was. The storm raging outside had finally decided to unleash its fury after threatening to all day. Given the choice of being drenched attempting to get home and another drink, the ale won hands down.

"Here you go," Carl said, sliding a draft down the bar. It came to a stop squarely in front of its new owner. "You seem a little preoccupied tonight, Mikey. Can I lend an ear? It's what we bartenders are known for."

"I am a bit out of it. It isn't the beer either," Mike replied, his sly smile accentuated by a wink. "It's personal. I don't normally air my dirty laundry in public."

Carl glanced around the bar. "No worries about being overheard tonight. I think you might be the only one crazy enough to brave this weather. The reports have been issuing warnings all day. I almost didn't open. Let me guess... it has to do with a woman."

Mike half-chuckled under his breath. "Doesn't it always?" he answered. "This is a one-that-got-away problem. Believe it or not, I was almost engaged." He pulled out a small black box, slamming it on the table.

"I take it that's the ring?" Carl questioned, side-eyeing the tiny package. He continued drying glasses with a white towel. Slow evenings were common enough, but bad weather always dialed down the participation meter. Most of his patrons had a beer or two waiting in their fridges; they came to his place for the company. Camaraderie only stretched so far in the face of a night like they were having. That didn't mean he wasn't able to make the most of a bad situation. If he wasn't selling anything, he was determined to catch up on a few chores around the place. It only made sense.

"Yup," Mike answered, laughing. "It was the most cliché moment of my life. I had big news. She had big news. Being a gentleman, I let her go first... big mistake." His head stopped shaking as his mug neared his lips.

"Let me guess; her news wasn't about being in love and wanting to take things to the next level?" Carl said, one eyebrow arched.

"She had big plans. A job offer meant her career was taking off in all new directions," Mike explained. He gulped back an oversized mouthful of beer.

"And none led to a life with you?" Carl asked, his focus still on drying the glassware.

"Not a one," Mike admitted.

"Did you ask her?" the bartender inquired.

"After her big news, I didn't have the guts," Mike replied. "I congratulated her. She was short for time with all the packing left to be done. She gave me a kiss goodbye, which was more of a bird peck. That was it. The love of my life walked out the door and didn't look back. That was five years ago."

"Five years?!" Carl exclaimed, pausing his chores. "And you are still pining over it now?"

"Yeah," Mike replied. "Thing is, after all this time, I heard from her. Knollville isn't as small as it once was and it seems she has a rather impressive job offer right here in town. She might be moving back." A huff and hiccup escaped his parted lips at the same time. "She acted like nothing had ever happened."

"I'll give you a bit of advice, mate," Carl offered. "Exes are exes for a reason. Tread lightly. This woman could turn your heart inside out in a split second."

"Yeah, I know," Mike agreed, chuckling. "Why do you think I'm here doing all this soul-searching?" He held up his mug, beer swooshing from side to side. In one long chug, its contents drained away. "Ah!"

"Another?" Carl asked, already filling a new stein. He'd seen enough broken-hearted men in his lifetime to know when asking was merely a formality.

"Sounds good," Mike answered. "I need to forget Penny once and for all. This is the best way I know how. She won't be lurking at the bottom of a brew, that's for sure."

"Another woman might help," Carl suggested. "The best way to forget one girl is to get on top of another." His lips curled up in a sly grin. "A tried and true solution for most men's heartaches. Take it from me, go out on a few dates."

"If another woman walks through that door," Mike replied, "I will gladly take her home tonight."

As if on command, the front door creaked open. The wind howled in the background, its acknowledgment of the pledge that had just been made.

Carl laughed, rounding the bar. He smacked his patron on the back. "Looks like you got your wish," he joked.

Mike smacked his forehead. The woman in question was a walking disaster and not all of it could be attributed to the storm. Drenched, head-to-toe, she looked like something the cat dragged in. He was going to need a few more drinks to get out of this one.

Chapter Four

Seren fought with the door. The wind gusted twice as hard undoing all the work she had put into closing it. Rain pelted sideways, continuing to drench her already soaked attire.

"I'll get that," a man called out. "You come in and have a seat. It's a mess out there tonight. This might be the storm of the year."

Seren shivered. Gladly accepting the man's offer, she headed to an empty spot at the bar. That in itself was no easy feat. Puddles formed as she walked, leaving the floor slippery beneath what was left of her stockings. Another slip and fall wasn't needed to make things worse.

Being perched on a bar stool was the perfect vantage point to survey the rest of the room. The bar had only one other patron. At least that limited the number of people bearing witnesses to her breakdown. Neither of the two men would probably even notice. Bars were where people went when they hit rock bottom -- to drink their woes away.

"That storm is a bad one," the bartender said, shaking his head. "You look like you could use a drink. What can I get you?"

Seren licked a few stray drops off her lips. "Have anything that can make me forget a really bad day?" She flashed a smile, not that anyone would notice. The drips falling off her nose stole the show. One hand swatted at them, to no avail. As soon as one was gone a new one began its descent to replace it.

"We have lots for that," he answered, a welcoming grin forming at the corners of his mouth. "That's what most folks come to a place like this for. How about a whiskey on the rocks?"

"Sounds good," Seren agreed. She opened her purse, her hand frantically searching its contents. An array of items fell onto the bar. "Hold on. I'm sorry. I must have left my wallet at work." Her purse slammed down on the bar top, her head following suit.

"I got it," the man a few seats down blurted out. "Give the lady a drink, Carl."

"Whatever you say, Mikey," the bartender answered, filling a glass with an amber liquid.

"Thank you," Seren mumbled, taking an over sized gulp. She winced, feeling the burn from her throat to her stomach. She'd never been much of a drinker. She eyed the remaining contents. That was about to change.

"I'm Mike." He slithered down several stools in one swift motion, his hand extended.

"Seren," she replied, trying to dry her hands on soaked clothing. The bartender offered a towel.

"As in Serenity?" Mike asked, trying to keep the conversation alive, but withdrawing his previous gesture.

"Serendipity, actually," she answered. The towel dried the final drops from her face, before rubbing through drenched bushy black hair.

"That's an unusual name," Mike commented. "I bet there's a story that goes with it."

"There is," Seren admitted, "but it's a rather long one and I'm not sure you'd find it all that interesting."

"Until this storm lets up, it's you, me, and Carl." He pointed with his glass to each of them as he spoke. "We aren't going anywhere. We could sit here in silence, wallowing in our problems, I suppose. I think I'd prefer to hear your story, though. At the very least it might take our minds off of things."

Seren's lips curled up for the first time that day. "Okay. My father was Celtic and my mother practiced Wicca."

"That's an interesting combination," Carl stated. "It doesn't explain how you got your name, though."

"I'm getting to that," Seren replied. "I did say it was a long story." The thoroughly soaked towel fell in heap on the bar.

"That you did," Mike agreed. He held up his empty glass, looking for a refill.

"They met in New Orleans at Mardi Gras," Seren continued. "It was love at first sight and a week-long whirlwind romance." Her eyes glistened; flecks of gold in a pit of tar.

"Rather ironic," Carl blurted out, tossing the drenched towel in a bin ready for the laundry service. That was one job he didn't do himself. Cutting corners on sanitation was the one thing no bar owner should ever do. "You stumbling in here... a bar named Mardi Gras."

Seren glanced around, her eyes widening at the sight of the logo on the window. "I didn't even notice," she muttered. "The storm had my full attention." She chuckled. A hockey puck paid better attention to details. Numerous times she passed by that very spot, not once noticing the name of the establishment. A chill ran down her spine, urging for a second sip of alcohol to warm it away. She didn't hesitate to comply.

"So, what happened next?" Carl asked, hunching over the bar to offer his full attention.

"Their vacations were ending, but their love wasn't," Seren answered. "Their families didn't agree with their involvement. So they decided to elope."

"After a week?!" Mike exclaimed. "That's a little reckless, isn't it? Can people really fall for each other that fast?"

"I admit love at first sight doesn't happen often, but it does happen," Seren argued. "Their love was perfect. They found a local to perform the ceremony, taking both of their beliefs into consideration. After, when they were leaving, a strange man approached them dressed head-to-toe in white. With a tip of his hat, he offered his congratulations. To commemorate the occasion, he presented them with a rather odd wedding present."

"A man they didn't know gave them a gift?" Mike asked. He shook his head, tossing back another glass of frosty brew. "What was it?"

"A coin," Seren answered.

"That's it?" Mike scoffed. "A coin? How is that a wedding gift? I can think of a lot of better things to give newly-weds."

"He claimed he wanted them to have the best possible life together," Seren explained. "Supposedly, he enchanted it with a rare and powerful magic."

"So it's a lucky coin," Carl mumbled. "You don't hear much about those in these parts."

Seren smiled. "My parents had it encased in a type of shadow box, claiming they never wanted to use its abilities. As long as it stays inside, its power remains untouched."

"This story is odd," Mike blurted out, "But not using something like that is really strange. If I had an insta-luck piece, it wouldn't be leaving my pocket. That is the one thing we could all use."

"Although they had different beliefs, there was one thing my parents both agreed on; with the practice of magic comes not just benefits, but also consequences," she explained. "In essence, by using the coin, they believed they were creating a debt that one day would have to be paid. Neither one of them were willing to take the chance it might cost them something important."

"How does your name fit in?" Mike asked, growing tired of the supernatural talk.

"Serendipity, by definition, basically means good luck that happens by chance," she replied. "My parents believed having me was the only luck they needed, and it came without a price tag... the way it should. They're both gone now." Her lips curled down to match a blank stare.

"Is that the coin?" Carl asked, pointing to a small box sitting on the bar.

"Oh!" she exclaimed. "It must have fallen out when I was looking for my wallet." She picked it up, staring at the shiny surface begging to be released. "That's it."

"If you are having such a bad day," Mike said. "Maybe you should open it..."

Seren glanced over at him. "Maybe I should..."

Gazing off in the distance she envisioned her own wedding, a dream from her childhood that had never been realized. The one thing she wanted, more than anything else, was exactly what her parents had; love at first sight, the whirlwind romance, and a New Orleans wedding.

Her mother and father might have told her time and again it wasn't as easy as it looked. That didn't matter. She knew better. Their lives had been filled with everything hers wasn't, and they kept the coin under wraps to boot.

A smile graced her lips. They weren't there to scold her like a little girl anymore. The coin was in her hands and she could do what she pleased with it.

Chapter Five

Serendipity pulled the covers down over her eyes, just enough to glance around. Blurred vision focused on a room she had never seen before. Her mouth opened, a tiny gasp escaping. Luckily, It wasn't loud enough to wake the man beside her.

Her brain caught up to her eyes, remembering details of the previous evening. It had been quite some time since she dated, let alone slept with anyone. Her dry lips cracked as a smile tried to form. It had been a while since she had been out for a few drinks as well, a few being a rather large understatement.

She glanced to the side, moving as slowly as possible. If this was a one-night stand, exiting before he woke up was better than being tossed out on her butt. There was nothing like a mood killer to start the day off on the wrong foot.

"Hey," Mike said, his lips smacking together. He covered his eyes with the crease of his elbow. "What time is it?"

"Early," Seren replied. "I was trying not to wake you. I have a big day at work." She gathered her clothes from where they lay strewn across the floor. "I'll grab a cab home."

"You sure?" Mike muttered, a snore tapering off his words.

"Yeah, um." Seren bit her bottom lip. "Where am I? I need to tell the cab driver."

Mike rubbed his face. "The apartments on Porter." One eye half opened. He handed her a fistful of bills to pay for the ride.

"Forty-two Porter?!" she exclaimed.

"Yeah," Mike answered, yawning. "You know them?"

"Yeah, I live here," Seren stated.

"You live in this building?" Mike asked, sitting up. He fell over, rubbing his temples. "I'm 207."

"Upstairs one floor," Seren replied. "Odd we never met before, isn't it?"

Mike's answer came in the form of a loud snore. This time, he was out for the count. That left the perfect opportunity for an escape.

"I'll see myself out," Seren whispered, throwing the rest of her clothes on in the hallway.

Up until then, doing a walk of shame was one thing she'd managed to avoid in life. Seren opted for the stairs as the best choice to make it to her apartment without controversy. Going up a single flight was much better than strutting through town in disarray. For once, coincidence was on her side, allowing her to easily dodge the incoming bullet. That sort of luck hadn't happened in a long time. To make things even sweeter, not a single person saw her.

She let out the air she'd been holding in at the sound of the door latching closed behind her. It was good to be home, especially without incident. Her keys landed with a clank on a glass side table. The contents of her other hand joined them.

Seren bit her lip, staring at the money. Mike had given it to her for a cab; a cab she didn't need to take. She scratched her head. That was a rather large oops; one she'd have to take care of later, considering he was asleep in his apartment. Pounding on his door to return it was worse than taking it in the first place.

Seren headed straight for the shower. Clothes peeled off quickly, hitting the trash can. There was no use trying to save them after the beating they took the previous day at the hands of the storm. Her feet, still aching from blisters and bruises, tested the ceramic tile before agreeing to step onto its lukewarm surface.

She heaved a sigh of relief as hundreds of tiny droplets hit her hair, soaking it. Steam filled the room, heat seeping into every pore of her skin. Her eyes rolled back. Her body relishing in the feeling which was a million times better than being caught in a torrential downpour. She delighted in every second. Her body begged for a few minutes more in the warming massage. Those urges, were denied, though. The dial turned easily in her hand, the water flow ceasing to a few drips. Today was an important day, one she couldn't be late for.

Water pooled around her feet as she stood in front of the mirror. Her own hazy image blurred behind a layer of fog. A towel wiped it away in a single streak, leaving behind a new unexpected figure in its wake.

Her eyes watered, at the sight of her father, head shaking in disapproval. Countless times she had been subjected to that same look. Any moisture left on her sizzled. It wasn't the first time a lifetime of suppressed rage was served up on a silver platter. The dish was bitter-sweet, but delicious just the same. Each swallow calmed the beast. Her hand lashed out, wiping the glossy surface one more time, but still unable to remove his face from her sight.

"Is this my punishment?" she muttered to her own reflection. "Are you haunting me now?"

She turned around, glancing over her shoulder at the large image tattooed on her back: a cross meant to remind her of all that her father stood for. More than a handful of his rules had been broken in the past day.

Guilt was her least favourite emotion and as unavoidable as any other. It was a feeling that couldn't be snuffed out altogether, but putting it on the back burner for a while was a temporary fix. Just as a bandage could heal a wound, pushing shame and regret into her stomach crated an opportunity for her body to fully digest it.

A white blow-dryer aimed at the mirror. With a simple flip of the switch, both her father's apparition and the rest of the fog disappeared from hindering her view. All that remained was her own image staring back, and it wasn't judging her. The hot air changed directions, starting the work for which it was meant.

The counter was always cluttered with an array of hair beauty products, each one promising better control, easier styling, and less frizz. None of them had ever actually fulfilled the promises they made. At best, if she left her hair down, she'd resemble a poodle on a bad hair day with or without the expensive bottles of oils and conditioners. She opted for without. There was already enough of a mess to clean up without adding to it.

A scowl was already in place before the brush made first contact. Knots were the worst. One overzealous stylist or another, herself and her mother included, had pulled out more than her fair share of hairs over the years. The pain of each tangle was etched into her memories. Her eyes clenched together tightly, preparing for the worst as she pulled down.

"Ow!" Seren flicked her hand from the wrist, back and forth, not having been prepared for the bang against the counter. The brush hadn't found one tangle to become stuck on. The unruly curls that made up her normal bird's nest had vanished. Not even a kink was left behind. Her hand shook as it went for a second pass with the same results. The blow-dryer roared its approval, whisking away all remaining moisture.

She glanced into the mirror. The eyes staring back at her sparkled with surprise. Her head tilted from one side to the other. This was the straightest her hair had ever been. It happened without styling aids, without specialty products. A chuckle escaped slightly parted lips.

Wood scraped against wood as a rarely used drawer opened. It's contents issued a new challenge... makeup. More particularly, liquid eyeliner was the adversary.

An array of fashion magazines lay strewn about every room of the apartment. Each contained any number of models, with perfectly formed liner strokes aiding their natural beauty. Seren had tried, on numerous occasions, to reproduce those exact looks. Each attempt failed miserably. The outcome was on par with social media nailed-it memes showing side by side views of the original picture and one humorously ridiculous attempt at rivaling it.

Her first strokes were never even. Going back to try to fix them only made things worse, thickening the lines. Before the makeover was completed, the only model she ended up resembling was a raccoon in a hunting magazine.

Still with a few ounces of self-confidence left over from her hair, Seren grabbed a black liner and popped the cap off. Her mouth formed an oval shape, stretching her skin down as much as possible. The black liquid went to work on the top eyelid. For the first time ever, the line was flawless. Not wanting to smudge her impeccable work, the hair-dryer roared hot air in its direction, removing all traces of moisture. A blink tested out the liner's durability, leaving behind no traces of smearing. Then came the real test: the second eye. For the experiment to be hailed a success, the two had to match.

Her grin expanded acknowledging the stranger staring back at her. The woman in the mirror was as beautiful as she had ever hoped to be. No matter what else happened, it was already the best day of her life. Nothing was going to bring her down from this newfound high.

The smile faded as fast as it had appeared. She'd completely forgot about the files. If Mr. Burns made it to the office before her, she could kiss that promotion goodbye, along with her current job. Unfortunately, her boss was a renowned early riser. There was a good chance he was already at the office.

In a split-second decision, she grabbed the stick. Inserting it into her computer, she emailed it's contents directly to his personal account. That was the best solution, for the moment. With the bus schedule the way it was, there was no telling how long it would take to get to work. At the most, she'd maybe arrive a few minutes early. A pink tongue darted out, wetting her lips... unless.

Seren glanced over her shoulder at the side table. Mike had offered her the money for a cab. If she used it for one, she wasn't technically taking advantage of him. Her thumbs twiddled in indecision. Of course, if she ended up with the promotion, she could thank him and pay him back later at Mardi Gras.

Chapter Six

Jeff tossed a quarter in the air and caught it again, slamming it on the backside of his free hand. He jotted down another tick in the heads column. Tails wasn't performing quite as well.

The copier humming in the background wasn't enough to break his concentration. The quarter flipped between his fingers in a hypnotic pattern.

While it was true, money was the root of all evil, the coin he was thinking about took things to a whole new level. What was the connection between the coin found by the dead thief and Truly? She was in a coma and he was dead. There were no answers coming from the only two who actually knew the truth. Fortunes were Truly's thing, not lucky coins. He pursed his lips together, pushing them out slightly.

"I know that look," Miranda said, taking a seat across from him at her desk. She handed him a paper cup filled with his favourite dark roast blend.

"What?" Jeff complained, tossing her a few bills to pay for the day's coffee. He hadn't done that nearly enough the past while. His mind had been far too preoccupied with other issues. More often than not, he took for granted his partner remembering to bring the java in.

"You know what," Miranda replied. "You are stewing over something, and it probably isn't even anywhere on our list of assignments."

"Yeah, you got me," Jeff admitted. His feet fell from their resting spot on his desk; his chair scooting forward. "It's the coin. I can't get it out of my head."

"The coin?" Miranda repeated, rolling her eyes. "What coin? Sometimes, I can't even begin to understand your thought processes."

"The coin," Jeff answered with an emphasis on the word the. "The one found by the body of the thief in the park."

"I thought we agreed the Truly case was closed," Miranda scoffed. "She is in a coma. Her assailant is dead. Why are you still harping on this?"

"Something isn't sitting right," Jeff argued. "If it was a lucky coin, it didn't work very well for the dead guy."

"So it was a dud," Miranda joked. "Just because we work in the basement paranormal division doesn't mean everything we come across will be of a supernatural background."

"Right," Jeff agreed. "But... check this out." He handed his partner a list.

"What am I looking at?" Miranda questioned.

"That's a list of what Truly had in her possession when she left the station," Jeff replied. "This is a list of what was found on her. Do you see what is missing?"

"A coin," Miranda mumbled. She held up a single finger. "But, we knew he was a thief and she had no other money on her. They scuffled and he stole it. Truly fell and hit her head, resulting in the coma and the guy..."

"Ran face first into concrete," Jeff blurted out. "How does anyone do that?"

"It was dark," Miranda answered, tossing the papers on her desk. "He couldn't see where he was going and took a wrong turn. It was an accident." She bit her upper lip, wishing she hadn't used the word accident. Her partner rarely believed in those.

"I thought that at first, too," Jeff said. Putting his pencil behind one ear, he rifled through a stack of papers. "So, I took the liberty of looking up what safety precautions were used by the company doing the paving. They are liable for damages if anyone gets hurt, after all. It didn't seem plausible that there wasn't some form of lighting."

"Why would you do that?" Miranda asked, her nose scrunching up. "It was a closed case."

"As a concerned officer," Jeff started, "I wanted to be sure the rest of Knollville was safe. We can't have people stumbling in cement and dying everyday, can we?"

"I suppose not." The lines between Miranda's brows deepened, her lips twitching at the sides. She knew exactly where this was going and it was a direction she didn't want to follow.

"As it turns out, they used glow-in-the-dark materials on top of a few solar lights to make sure the area was clearly visible, even at night," Jeff said, rounding the desks. He dropped another paper in his partner's lap.

"So," Miranda said, "you are saying he should have seen it. Maybe he did and didn't think it was still wet. He could have tripped."

"There is no way he should have fallen the way he did," Jeff stated, holding one finger in the air. "Also, he didn't make any attempt to get out of the cement. It wouldn't have been an instant dry situation. Why didn't he try to get up?"

"How do we know he didn't?" Miranda questioned.

Jeff pulled pictures out from behind his back. "There are no marks in the surface, except for under him. That means he didn't move after he originally fell. He simply lay there and died."

"I'll admit that is strange," Miranda agreed. "But I still don't see how the coin fits in."

"I'm working on that," Jeff mumbled. "I don't know the answer yet, but I am going to figure it out."

"Or die trying?" Miranda scoffed.

"I thought you agreed to keep an open mind," Jeff complained. "That was part of transferring to this department."

"I signed up more to keep your two feet on the ground," Miranda replied. "Okay, I give. You are going to tell me anyway. What type of coin is it?"

"I don't know," Jeff answered, returning to his chair with a thump. "I've spent hours looking up different coins and I haven't found one that matches yet."

"You'll end up needing glasses if you keep staring at that screen," Miranda snapped. "We have a stack of complaints to investigate. I suggest we start with this one."

Jeff huffed, glancing over the file. "A cat lady," he complained. "That isn't even something a rookie in our old department would be wasting time looking into. Why not send animal control?"

"Because," Miranda answered, lingering on the word. "There is some talk that the cats are actually frogs."

Jeff turned his head slowly, his upper lip in an arch. "So, a frog lady. Still sounds like an animal control issue to me."

"No," Miranda argued. "Apparently, she is turning frogs into cats. We need to have her reverse the process. It violates one of the paranormal city ordinances."

"Why does the city care if they are frogs or cats?" Jeff asked. "Either way they are still animals."

"If you spent more time on our job and less chasing the ghosts of closed cases, you might know." Miranda crossed her arms over her chest with a huff. "I'll explain it, this time."

"Thank you," Jeff replied with a head bow.

"When we were in the academy, we were taught about how serial criminals start out small and grow over time to bigger and better feats," Miranda said.

Jeff nodded his agreement. "Evolving is pretty standard stuff for criminals."

"That's what the city is afraid of," Miranda declared.

"You mean instead of frogs to cats, it would be people to frogs?" Jeff asked. "That would make a strange cycle... people to frogs; frogs to cats."

Miranda chuckled. "It's our job to see to it that never happens," she said. "How about we stop by and check out the cat lady, then I buy you lunch and we can make a game plan?"

Jeff chuckled. "Sounds good. How'd you know I was hungry?"

"How couldn't I know?" Miranda replied. "I can hear your stomach grumbling from over here."

Chapter Seven

"Mr. Burns would like a word," Ms. Parker bellowed, despite being only inches from her ear. She turned to leave, pausing before actually walking away. "Now!"

Seren's chair jerked backward, knowing she was expected to follow. Her head hung down, eyes averted from the gawks of co-workers. This was how cattle felt being led to slaughter. Their peers knew what was in store for them and felt remorse, but none of them had the power to change the outcome. Trying could have wound them up on the chopping block as well.

Sucking in air, she knocked on the dark wood door. At least she looked fabulous for her final day.

"Come," a man's voice instructed.

Seren paused before entering. The realization she'd never met Mr. Burns before blocked her way. To be more accurate, she had never even seen a glimpse of him. For a while, she was convinced he didn't actually exist and Ms. Parker was in charge. It made sense with the way her pointy nose stuck up at the tip, a side effect from it being lodged in other people's business. This was the moment of truth. She was about to find out who really ran the show.

All preconceived notions of what lay behind the wooden door flew out the window the moment the door opened. Her expectations of an old-fashioned, large desk strewn with papers and half-organized clutter were blown away by a modern open-concept room. There were no book shelves or filing cabinets. A single metal desk sat as the focal point of the room, surrounded by bare windows with an unobstructed view of the happenings of Knollville below.

The latest technology came with a high price tag; too high for Seren. Even if she wasn't up-to-date with the latest gizmos and gadgets, she still knew Mr. Burns's computer was top of the line. Its sleek lines and small frame created its own form of camouflage. From what she could tell from a distance, it appeared to be a hybrid cross between a laptop and a notebook. Of course, that was just a guess. It was difficult to say for sure, especially with limited knowledge in the field.

Her employer was also a bit of a surprise, appearing much younger than most stereotypical men of power. His dark hair was perfectly styled without even a hint of grey. Not even his well-groomed beard showed any signs of age. A perfectly tailored designer-label suit enhanced his trim physique.

Mr. Burns stood, hand in one pocket, the other dancing across a virtual keyboard. "So you are Serendipity," he commented, lips puckered. "Do you know why I called you here?"

Seren cleared her throat. "It's about the files from this morning," she answered. There was no use beating around the bush. Dragging out a firing was only prolonging the embarrassment that came with it.

Mr. Burns glanced up at her for the first time. "Let me share something with you," he said. "I built this business on lip service." He paused, watching her. "Do you know what that means?"

Serendipity felt perspiration forming on her brow. Accepting one's fate and dealing with it were two very different things. "I-I," she began to stutter.

"Loyalty, intuition and perseverance. Those three things equal service," he blurted out. "If you have those qualities, you are sure to succeed."

"I'm not sure how that applies to me, sir" Seren squeaked, her fingers tugging on the bottom of her shirt.

"This morning when you emailed me those files, you showed me all of those qualities," Mr. Burns answered. "At first, it took me aback. It isn't, after all, our company's normal practice."

"I know, sir," Seren replied. "After yesterday, I wanted to make sure the same thing didn't happen again."

"Yes," Mr. Burns said. "Yesterday took us all by surprise." He shook his head. "No one had any clue our client was going to show up so early and hastily depart before the office even opened for the day."

Seren opened her mouth, prepared to question Ms. Parker's claims that her tardiness had thrown everything off kilter, but thought better of it. Wherever this meeting was going, she needed to ride it out.

"Out of everyone working on this deal, you were the only one with the forethought that it could happen again," Mr. Burns continued. "Your email saved the deal."

"It did?" Seren questioned, a grin forming in the corners of her lips.

"It did," Mr. Burns replied. "I've looked at your file and have gone over the application you submitted for our upper-level team. I admit I was going to outsource, but I've changed my mind. The job is yours if you want it."

Seren's jaw fell open. This was a complete one-eighty. She'd expected to be fired, not promoted.

"Well, don't just stand there gawking," Mr. Burns ordered. "Go fetch your personal items and get settled into your new office. That is, if you still want the job."

"Yes," Seren blurted out, her grin transforming into a full smile. "Thank you. This means so much to me." Realizing not only was the meeting over, but that she was blabbering, she turned to make a quick exit. The moment the door shut, her feet moved quickly in time, performing a victory dance of their own.

Seren graced the route to her new corner office with the best strut in her arsenal. Her hips swung as she glided by each employee, head raised high for the first time. The only comments made were those born from jealousy. Those she could handle. Even her parents would have been proud of her for this accomplishment.

Chapter Eight

There weren't a lot of items needing to be collected and moved. Seren wasn't a picture and plant type of employee. Those things merely added to the work clutter that was bound to multiply swiftly on any desk.

A blank plate holder on the entrance to her new office confronted her. In the coming days, a brass attachment with her name engraved on it would be added. Her lips puckered, allowing air to escape slowly. This was by far her finest moment.

The handle was cool to the touch and turned easily within her grasp. She bit her bottom lip, wondering what lay ahead for her. Her heart rate quickened, anticipation drying out her mouth. Hopefully a water cooler was part of the deal.

The permanent smile that had graced her lips since hearing of her promotion spread like wildfire. Her mostly empty box slid on a functional desk. The sight of drawers and shelves relieved her fears of a spotless work station similar to Mr. Burns's. Something like that she never would have been able to pull off.

Seren took a seat in her new executive chair, pushing back to feel the full extent of its cushioning. Never before had she felt such luxury from merely sitting. Every desk drawer opened, all of them empty, except one containing a remote. Her eyes darted from side to side. There was no way she wasn't going to give it a whirl. Her fingers ran over buttons, pushing one and then the other. It was her back that reaped the rewards in the form of heat and massaging vibrations.

Her lips parted, allowing a low chuckle to escape. This was too good to be true. It certainly couldn't be considered work, being more like a trip to the spa. The chair swivelled facing the view outside. She leaned back enjoying every sensation that came with her new position. Lost in her own thoughts, she almost missed a faint knock.

"Hello," a woman called out, peeking in the slightly cracked door. "Ms. Parker sent me."

Seren spun back around. "Hello. How can I help you?"

"Actually, I was sent to help you," she said. "I'm Timone, your new secretary."

"Secretary," Seren repeated. "Okay. I didn't realize I was getting my own assistant. I didn't see a desk out there..."

"No," Timone blurted out, pushing a pair of glasses up the bridge of her nose. "We all work on the first floor. I've set up your devices so I am only a button away through the office network. Once you get the hang of things, it is quite easy." She placed several items on the desk. "This is your phone. I am programmed in with my work and personal contacts." She pointed to different logos on the background. "Just press the one that goes with the time of day. I'll answer."

"Why would I need you outside of work hours?" Seren questioned, glaring at the screens.

"I am here to make you successful," Timone answered. "To be a success you have to look the part. My job doesn't end when we exit the building. You represent the company now twenty-four hours a day. I will be available anytime to help pick out appropriate wardrobes, hairstyles, vacations... you name it. I'll also take care of all reservations and appointments." She placed a tablet on the desk. "This is your personal schedule. It is also uploaded to each of the other devices. I have set warning alarms for two hours before events."

"That's very thorough," Seren stated. "Thank you." She glanced over the woman, assessing her from head-to-toe. She wore a blue suit over a crisp white button-down shirt and a red scarf; all the perfect makings of a stereotypical airplane stewardess, right down to the functional pumps on her feet.

"It's my job," Timone replied, attempting a smile. Her lips only managed to curl up slightly in the corners, a side effect of either the tightness of the bun her brown hair was pulled up into or plastic surgery. It was hard to tell which.

The walls vibrated, shaken by a woman's voice from the hallway. Whoever she was, she wasn't happy. Timone opened the office door providing a full view of the pretty woman. If she hadn't been complaining bitterly to Ms. Parker about something, she could have passed for any member of the senior team. Not only did she dress the part, but her blonde hair was also tied back in the office's signature bun. Her arms rose then flapped down at her sides. A few locks of golden hair fell loose as her head shook in denial.

"Mr. Burns is a busy man!" Ms. Parker yelled. "I am sorry, but he won't see you. The position has been filled."

"Who is that?" Seren asked.

"That," Timone answered, looking down over her glasses, "is the woman you beat out for this job. Her name is Penny.

From what I understand, her flight was delayed and she missed her interview. She would have been a shoo-in, if she had made it. I heard she came a long way, too. Her bad luck is your good luck, I suppose. That's the way the world goes round."

"Yeah," Seren muttered. "Luck."

"I'll let you settle in," Timone said, more interested in what was happening outside the office than in it. "If you need me, I'm just a button away." She scurried off to join other employees forming an audience to the event that was underway.

Seren opened her purse. Her hand plunged in, but instead of fumbling around came directly in contact with the item she was looking for. A shiny coin emerged. She flipped it in the air, catching it on the way back down. Her lips grazed across its smooth surface. The other woman's name might have been Penny, but she was the one with the lucky coin.

Chapter Nine

Mike opened and shut the tiny ring box several times before stashing it away in his side pocket. He reached for the frosted mug to drown away his feelings.

"Still brooding over the girl?" Carl asked. "Did you talk to her? Last time we spoke, you said she was moving back."

"I haven't heard a peep since that one call," Mike admitted. "I thought for sure she would phone me the second she landed. Maybe it was all wishful thinking on my part."

"I thought you were seeing that other one." Carl said, pouring a couple drafts for the local afternoon crowd hovering around a television at the other end of the bar. He slid them down the line, each ending up perfectly in the hand of the patron it was meant for.

Mike huffed. "We are... sort of. If you call getting drunk and screwing a relationship."

"You don't like her?" Carl questioned, leaning over the bar. "You seem to get along well."

"It sounds bad. I know," Mike replied, "but I don't actually know her. I'm usually half-baked when she arrives. She's a light weight, so it doesn't take her long to catch up. Most of the time she mumbles on about her parents and how much she loves New Orleans. How anyone can love a place they haven't visited, I'll never know."

"What's it been, a week?" Carl pried.

"Almost," Mike admitted. "I probably should break it off, but..."

"It's better than being alone," Carl said, finishing his sentence.

"Yeah." Mike's eyebrows arched and fell. A final swig of beer swirled around at the bottom of his glass before emptying into his mouth. He gulped it back. "I suppose it is."

Carl motioned toward the door. There was no need to look. Serendipity had arrived. He patted his pocket, making sure the ring box was tucked away and out of sight.

"Hey," Seren said, brushing her lips against the back of Mike's head. "How was your day?"

"Same as always," he replied, without emotion. He held up two fingers. Carl nodded his understanding. Drinks appeared without a word spoken.

"I've been thinking," Seren started, allowing the ice cold drink to wet her lips. "It's the perfect time to take a vacation. We should plan a trip."

"Sure," Mike said, chuckling. "Why not? It's not like we have jobs or anything to worry about." He guzzled back the contents of the latest round, ordering another before he finished.

"It could be a weekend getaway," Seren suggested.

"Vacations are nice," Carl said. "Anywhere in particular you are thinking of heading to?"

"Mardi Gras is good enough for me," Mike said, rolling his eyes. "no need to go any further."

Seren squealed. "That's exactly what I was thinking," she blurted out. "It's the perfect time of year."

Mike gazed into his glass at the frothy liquid. He walked right into that one. Mardi Gras, to him, meant the bar. If he hadn't already put away a few drinks, he might have realized to Serendipity it meant a trip to New Orleans. He bit his bottom lip and nodded. They'd just been discussing how much she loved it there before she walked in, too.

Carl patted him on the shoulder. "This one is on the house," he offered, placing a new frosted mug of ale on the bar.

He closed his eyes, tuning down her voice to no more than background noise. It wasn't that he wanted to be rude. It simply wasn't the night to listen to idle chatter about vacations he couldn't afford to take. Letting her down easy was going to be a real task, but somehow he'd find a way, sooner or later.

There was a conflict brewing within him. Part of him was pining for Penny; another told him to keep Seren around. His brain flipped a two-sided coin over and over, coming up with different outcomes on each turn. Men had gone mad over less. The time had come to make a decision. He gulped back his beer, sliding the glass back to Carl.

"I think we should call it a night," Mike suggested, offering his arm. "Would you care to join me for a nightcap?"

"Why thank you, kind sir," Seren replied, taking his offering. A seductive smile graced her lips.

Chapter Ten

Seren held her head. A bit too much drinking was, as of late, wreaking havoc on her body, the effects of which were beginning to wear thin. Constant headaches and morning spins were something she had hoped to one day experience with pregnancy. These ones weren't those, but merely a byproduct of consuming too much alcohol.

She glanced over at Mike, still sleeping. There had been enough nights in his bed now to know the short bursts of snorts meant he was still out for the count. Hot water, or the lack thereof after a certain time in their building, wasn't an issue for him.

One leg slipped out from under the covers, the other following suit. This was the part Seren despised, the hunt for her clothes. Trampling around someone else's apartment naked was uncomfortable, even if she was sleeping with him.

Tiptoeing gingerly around the bedroom, she gathered the few items that were there before heading down the hall. Had the lights been on, the task would have been much easier. As it was, she was relying on her sense of touch. Daylight savings time wasn't all it was cracked up to be. It certainly wasn't doing her any good waking up to darkness.

One foot became the search and rescue expert, sticking out in front of her to locate the missing. Figuring out what an item of clothing was by its feel alone was more complicated than it sounded. The latest find had her stumped. Part felt soft, perhaps cotton; another section was smoother. Her toes went in for another feel, this time hitting against something hard.

She fell to her knees, biting her lip to hold back a scream. Pain radiated from her baby toe. Whatever caused it deserved to be thrown at least once. Her hand took over, easily finding the pocket opening and diving inside. Her breath fluttered as a small box emerged in her grasp. She glanced over her shoulder, before heading to the bathroom for light to examine her find.

The black box stared back at her, begging to be opened. She alternated glances between the image in the mirror and the tiny object of interest. Her tongue rubbed against her bottom lip, trying to wash away the indecisiveness. It didn't work. One hand grasped the box and dropped it again multiple times.

Seren glanced at her watch. There wasn't any time to waste. If she was going to make it to work without being late, she needed to be out the door within fifteen minutes. Water splashed on her face from the open faucet. She kept both herself and the treasure in sight, quickly dressing. The moment had come. It was now or never. She opted for now.

"An engagement ring," she whispered. A smile twitched its way into the corners of her mouth. "Just like my parents. No... better than them."

Her hand shook as she removed it from its slot. Pride demanded a view of it on her finger. Admiration followed.

"It's perfect," she cooed.

She wiped a forming tear before it had the chance to fall. This was the happiest moment of her life and she owed it all to a little coin. Of course, she needed to let Mike ask her officially. Unfortunately, the ring disagreed with that plan.

"Oh, no!" she muttered. Her hand tugged and pulled, but the ring refused to budge.

Frantically, drawers and cupboards opened and closed. A sole bottle of lotion was her only hope. After thoroughly slathering it all over her hand, she attempted to pull the ring off a second time. Failure became her companion once again. The hand cream only made her grip more slippery.

Clenched fists left nail imprints in her palms. She was out of time. There was only one choice. She stashed the box in her own pocket, vowing to have the ring off before she saw Mike again. He didn't ever have to know. She could hide the ring somewhere in his apartment later for him to stumble upon.

Chapter Eleven

Jeff rubbed his stomach in a circular motion. "I'm starved," he said. "Good thing you're buying." He grabbed the menu, eyes darting over the selections. "That cat thing was hard work."

"You climbed a ladder," Miranda scoffed. "Saving a life should be ample reward."

"Cats in trees," Jeff said, "Not exactly detective work. There should have been a fine issued for wasting official police time. We need to work something out with animal services."

"Who would you like to give that fine to?" Miranda questioned. "The old lady who lives there?"

"I thought she was a witch," Jeff complained. "Couldn't she have found a way to get the kitty down?"

"That would have violated the city's *using magic in public* ordinances," Miranda explained. "She did the right thing calling in."

"She lied," Jeff argued. "There were never any frogs involved... just an ordinary cat afraid of heights."

"Would you have gone if she hadn't?" Miranda asked.

Jeff chuckled. "No."

"Exactly," Miranda blurted out. "Poor kitty would still be stuck in the tree. You have to give her points for originality. She reported herself in a way that got us there fast."

"Got you there fast," Jeff argued. "I was only there because of the deal we made."

"Says the guy who climbed the tree," Miranda snickered. "All I am saying is it was effective."

"I know what I'm having," Jeff declared, placing his menu back on the table.

"Let me guess... everything." Miranda rolled her eyes.

Jeff chuckled. "Close," he replied. "Any thoughts about the case?"

"You mean the coin?" Miranda questioned. "I'm not sure it qualifies as a case, yet."

Jeff huffed, folding his hands together on the table. "I am serious. My gut says we need to follow through. I just wish I knew how."

"If," Miranda started, "and this is a big if, the coin has some supernatural affiliation, there is one person in town we could stop by and have a chat with."

"You think Henry will have some intel?" Jeff asked. "I wasn't sure if we should bring him in on things just yet."

"Not Henry," Miranda squawked, "the psychic I met while we were investigating Truly. She has a museum of oddities... a paranormal collection of sorts. If anyone in Knollville knows about that coin, it's her. A short visit couldn't hurt, anyway. Did you bring the pictures?"

"Yeah." Jeff waved a file folder in the air. "I have it all right here and on my phone if need be. You really think this Zulana can help?"

"I don't know," Miranda admitted. "But if we are going to investigate this, we need to start somewhere."

Jeff laughed.

"What's so funny?" Miranda asked with an upward nod of her head.

"I was just thinking," Jeff answered, "you found our first official informant."

"I'm not sure I'd call her that," Miranda started.

Jeff silenced her with one hand. His head tilted, watching rings of water forming in the glass on the table. "Last time I checked we didn't have a dinosaur problem in Knollville."

"That would mean... an earthquake?" Miranda's upper lip raised. "I've never heard of this area having any."

"It doesn't... or didn't," Jeff agreed, "and shouldn't. My gut is telling me the coin is at least part of the problem."

"Then don't order too much and we can get back on the case," Miranda suggested.

"Don't worry," Jeff replied. "I eat fast."

Miranda shook her head. "I know. You can't blame me for trying, though."

Chapter Twelve

"Here are the reports you asked for," Timone said. The pile of folders fell from her arms. "Is that a diamond on your finger? Let me see!" She sidestepped the papers strewn about the floor.

Lies had a way of multiplying. One often became two and so forth down the line, infinitely increasing. Seren forced a smile over her lips, holding out her hand as if it were a natural response. "I didn't think anyone would notice."

Timone shook her head. "You have got to be kidding!" she exclaimed. "With the size of that rock, who could miss it? That man must love you in the worst way. Why haven't I heard about him before?" She glanced around the desk. "Not even one picture?"

"It's all very sudden," Seren replied. "Actually, the ring itself is a bit small. We need to have it resized, but I can't get it off my finger. You wouldn't happen to know a way?"

"Did you try butter?" Timone asked.

"No," Seren admitted. "Do you think that will work? Lotion was a bust."

"It couldn't hurt," Timone answered, shrugging her shoulders. "If that doesn't work, go to the jeweler it was bought from. I'm sure they have a way."

"Yeah," Seren grimaced. "I don't want to upset Mike. He doesn't know he misjudged the size."

"Hm," Timone huffed, her mouth twitching from side to side. "Let me call around and see what I can find out. A good manicurist might be able to help, too. You really should have your nails done if you are going to be sporting a rock that pretty. Give me an hour, we'll figure something out."

"Thanks," Seren mumbled, knowing her assistant was already gone. The woman had serious ninja skills that didn't belong in an office.

A glare of electricity exchanged between her eyes and the translucent stone. Its brilliance twinkled, even without direct light. The square cut stone dazzled her -- perfection worthy of royalty, but bought for her. The diamond was more valuable than anything else she had ever owned, save one thing: a shiny coin.

Even with the added luck, however, her assistant returned without a solid plan to remove the ring. Cutting either it off, or her finger, weren't viable options.

"What are you going to do?" Timone asked, her arms crossed over her chest.

"Tell him," Seren answered. "There isn't much else I can do at this point. I hope he understands."

"You could tell him you gained weight," Timone suggested. "That way he won't feel so bad for the sizing error."

Seren chuckled. That might have been an answer if Mike's feelings were the only problem. Still, she had little choice but to come clean. She glanced at her watch. If she hurried she could still catch him on his lunch break.

"I almost forgot," Seren lied, "I am supposed to meet him. Clear my schedule. I'll be back in an hour."

"Will do, boss," Timone said. "Take your time. It's not every day a girl gets engaged."

Seren fired off a quick grin. Hurrying through the building, she heard whispers here and there about the mystery man who had won her heart and her hand. News travelled fast, especially when it was fake. This mess wasn't going to be easy to clean up.

Chapter Thirteen

Seren hustled down the street, her body strutting with meaning in a hip-swinging power walk. There wasn't a moment to waste if she was going to catch Mike at the bar. She stumbled, catching her breath and her step as flashing red lights whizzed by her, sirens blaring.

"Must be an accident," a man beside her commented to no one in particular. He shrugged his shoulders before continuing on his way, as if nothing had happened. He was just one specimen, but represented humanity as a whole. The news blasted nasty details of atrocities and corruption three or more times a day, in one form or another. It was because of those reports people had become desensitized to the transgressions going on in their own backyard. Awful things were expected to happen and no one was surprised when they did.

Knollville might have been one of the last holdouts in a world consumed by violence, crime, and death, but all that had finally caught up. Accidents were becoming a normal part of life. Statistically speaking, they were on the rise and had been for numerous years. An evil crept in while the good citizens slept, worked, and turned the other cheek.

This year, however, odd mishaps seemed to have manifested in a more blatantly obvious manner. One in particular, involving a city bus driver, stuck out in her mind, having taken the life of her former landlord. She wanted to say it was regret, but truth-be-told it was more worry that filled the pit of her stomach. His death hadn't bothered her as much as it should have. Put plainly, the man was a blemish on the face of humanity and not the type that clears up, either. This was a zit that never came to a head, one that couldn't be popped to let all the pus out. No! Bernard festered under the skin, then, just when he appeared to be going away, BAM, he came right back in full force, until his death broke the pattern.

Things still weren't perfect in her building, but they were a lot better than they were before his untimely demise. That alone brought a feeling of relief rather than sadness. It was also quite a statement about her character. That was the first time she realized how little life actually meant.

Seren frowned. She heard about the accident on the local news and searched the papers for an obituary. There were none. From all accounts, Bernard lived and died alone. The odds of anyone attending his funeral were slim to none, save for maybe a mother, if he had one.

A twinge of anxiety resurfaced. In some ways they were a like. Seren often wondered who, if anyone, would come to mourn her. She bit her bottom lip, glancing down at the rock on her finger. At least there was Mike.

The flashing lights in the distance became more prevalent. Whatever had happened, hadn't taken place far from the bar. Her pace quickened, human nature demanding curiosity be satisfied. It wasn't disappointed. She arrived in time to see a black body bag being carried away by paramedics -- another victim to add to the statistics. Hopefully this one someone cared about.

Seren shook her head. That was more than enough time to waste on a stranger, especially a dead one. More pressing matters awaited attending to. She glanced over her shoulder at the dissipating crowd of gawkers. The accident itself could have been a bit of luck. There was a chance Mike was too preoccupied by the calamity and would let her off easy for trying on the ring.

Her eyes dropped to her hand. The afternoon sun caught the diamond in its sight. A prism of rainbows glared back at her from the door handle. The perfection stopped her in her tracks. Her parents had been completely wrong about the coin. They had been wrong about many things. If only they were alive to say *I told you so* to. The door swung open with authority.

"Carl," Seren called. "Is Mike still here? I need to speak with him. It is rather urgent."

At first glance, the bar looked closed. The only occupant was the bartender, hunched over and motionless. His gaze rose only just high enough to meet hers. A cold glare sent unsettling chills running up and down her spine, before leaving goosebumps on her arms as a warning something awful had happened. Carl remained silent; his lips pursed together.

It was said eyes were windows of the soul: an open book of emotions waiting to be read. If that was true, Carl's story was despair. There was no need to see tears. They had dried up before she arrived, turning the whites of his completely red, matching the blotchy patches of skin underneath them. He blinked -- a futile attempt to bat away the sadness.

"What's wrong?" she mumbled, unsure if she wanted an answer. A fluttering inside screamed for her to retreat -- run and never look back. Her body, however, had other plans. She needed to know what had happened in much the same manner as the crowd outside had. Curiosity should have been on the list of deadly sins. It wasn't only cats it killed. People only had one life, though, not nine.

Carl sniffled. "I guess you haven't heard," he whispered, dropping his gaze to his hands folded together on the bar.

"Is it about the accident?" Seren pointed to the window. A clean-up crew was all that remained, washing away any evidence left behind of life lost.

"Yeah." Carl bolted upright. "I've been saving this for a rainy day." He lifted a bottle of whiskey from its hiding place beneath the bar. "If you ask me it's the best ever made."

He slid two shot glasses in front of him before cracking the seal. The bottle rose to his nose in admiration of a well-crafted spirit, before pouring. He slid one across, motioning for Seren to join him.

"What happened?" she asked, inching closer. Her fingers wrapped around the tiny cup.

"Sit," Carl ordered. His shaking head stilled, tilting back to accept the amber liquid gift. A breath of air filled his lungs before huffing out quickly. "This isn't easy." His gaze fell to her hand. A look, once solemn, turned perplexed. "Where did you get that ring? Did Mikey give it to you?"

Seren exchanged glances between the bartender and her hand. She pulled it away to hide behind her back, leaving her shot glass on the bar. "What is going on?!"

Carl poured another shot and tossed it into his open mouth. Spirits slid down his throat of their own accord. "It's Mikey," he said. "He was in the accident. He didn't make it."

Seren's head shook furiously, her bottom lip trembling. "No! You are wrong!"

"I wish I were," Carl said. "I ran out as soon as I heard the noise. I was the one who found him on the road. A truck barreled him over while he was crossing."

"No!" Seren cried. "That's not possible. We were going to get married. We had plans to go to Mardi Gras in New Orleans. It was perfect... just like my parents. I know this can't be true, because I have luck on my side. I have the coin." Her gut wrenched. The truck might have hit Mike's body, but it was her psyche that was feeling the effects.

Carl shook is head, his eyes glued to his latest shot. "Maybe you do, but his ran out." He lifted his glass, motioning a cheers in the air. "To Mike. I'm going to miss him."

Seren backhanded the glass meant for her. Its contents splattered across the bar. The last thing she was prepared to do was drink to Mike's death.

Chapter Fourteen

Things had changed a smidge since Miranda's last visit to the fortune-teller's parlour, at least on the outside. Previously boarded up windows were now polished, with goods on display for anyone who passed by. An all new mystical market was booming with business in Knollville.

A blast of incense and perfumes assaulted her senses, sending her hand diving into a pocket in search of a tissue. Miranda sneezed into her elbow crease before it had a chance to return.

"Bless you," Jeff whispered. "Can I say that here?"

Miranda chuckled. "I don't think you'll offend anyone. There a many different types of blessings that range over any number of religions. I don't think the saying belongs to anyone in particular."

"It depends on the culture," Zulana said from the beaded curtain which led to the back. "Some believe the Pope originated the saying. Catholics like to be behind everything. Others believe it stops the soul from leaving the body. Then there are those who swear a good sneeze banishes evil from ones body. Superstitions..." Her eyes widened as she articulated the final word. "To each their own. What brings Knollville's finest back to my little shop? I'm not in trouble, I hope."

"No, not at all," Miranda replied. "This is my partner, Jeff. We have a few questions we'd like to ask you about some rare coins."

"Rare coins," Zulana echoed. "I am a collector of sorts, but I deal in magical oddities, not currency."

"We realize that. We believe these specific ones have been imbued with supernatural powers," Jeff added. "Have you heard of anything similar?"

"Supernatural powers?" Zulana repeated with a quizzical brow. "In what way?"

"Luck," Jeff answered.

Zulana chuckled a laugh as fake as her acrylic nails. "That is a rather broad topic. A penny found is considered lucky in one superstition -- in another -- only if you give it away. There are fountains and wishing wells to toss coins into to make your fondest dreams come true. Even Knollville has one of those. The English hide a coin inside their Christmas pudding; the person who finds one is expected to prosper throughout the coming year. Greeks believe all purses and wallets given as gifts must contain a lucky coin. The Chinese have their own version, complete with gaping holes in the center."

Jeff rubbed his jaw. "Are any of them true?"

Zulana laughed a little louder. "Anything one believes in strongly enough can be true. I can't answer any better than that. Mind over matter is as powerful as any mystical force."

"Are there any specific coins that could actually be considered magical?" Miranda questioned.

"Here," Jeff said, balancing a file on one knee while he pulled out a photograph. "Maybe this will help."

Zulana glanced at the image without touching the paper. Frown lines creased her otherwise perfect face. She headed to the door, turning the lock and flipping the sign to *Closed* simultaneously. "Come," she said, motioning to the back room. "Let's talk."

"You've seen one before," Jeff said, following her.

Zulana's hand pulled a pentagram charm back and forth on the chain around her neck. Her eyes dulled. "I have seen one similar, but this piece should not be turning up here. Knollville is not the place for such a thing."

"What can you tell us about it?" Miranda questioned.

"You said similar..." Jeff opened his mouth to continue, but was silenced by a hand.

"The coin I am speaking of may look different to each person," Zulana explained. "It can be whatever we expect it to be. Our mind fills in the details it wants to see."

"How do you know it is the same then?" Miranda asked.

"Because, to me, it looks the same as the other one did. Although I doubt what it reveals to me is the same as what it reveals to either of you," Zulana suggested. "Have you asked each other what is on the coin's surface?"

"That would be a rather odd thing to ask," Jeff replied.

"Of course, because you assume your partner can see exactly what you do," Zulana said. "But I bet if you compared notes, there would be some unexplained difference."

Miranda exchanged glances with her partner. "What else can you tell us about it?"

Zulana swivelled to face both the officers. "Rumours mainly. It is a story with roots deep in the magical community. You know the type -- tales that only circulate in certain crowds."

"Can you share it with us?" Jeff asked.

"Sit," Zulana commanded. A lighter flickered in her grasp, the flame shaking, afraid of the discussion it was summoned to bear witness to. She lit three candles, followed by a bundle of sage. Her hands waved the smoke toward her nostrils, bathing her in its cleansing abilities. "What do you know about mythology?"

"Not a lot," Jeff admitted. "I know as much as the next guy, mainly from movies."

"What about the River Styx?" Zulana asked.

"You had to pay the ferryman with a specific coins," Miranda blurted out. "You think that picture is one of them?"

"The story starts a few decades ago, although the exact dates I am unaware of," Zulana explained. "A talented young warlock climbed the ranks of the magical world with a never before heard of ability. Like many, he wanted to change the world -- leave his mark. That, combined with the arrogance of his youth, was a recipe for disaster."

"What did he do, steal the coins?" Miranda asked.

Zulana huffed. "If that had been all, things would have been fine. No, this fellow did something incredibly stupid."

"More stupid than stealing the underworld's currency? This should be good," Jeff scoffed.

Zulana inhaled the burning sage. "He not only pinched the coins, he imbued them with misappropriated dark powers."

"Taken from who?!" Miranda shrieked.

"Some say evil spirits trapped in the underworld; others the gods who rule there. Whichever doesn't matter. What does, is how upset the powers that be were." Zulana picked up the lid to a teapot and glanced inside. "Would you like some?"

"I'm fine," Jeff replied, inching forward in his chair. "What happened to the coins?"

"He gave them out as gifts," Zulana replied.

"What?!" Miranda exclaimed. "I don't get it."

"He attempted to turn dark forces into something good," Zulana suggested. "His heart was in the right place. His brain must have had the day off, though." She leaned back in her chair, teacup and saucer in hand.

"So it didn't work?" Jeff questioned.

"Oh, no, it worked." The cup clanged softly as she set it back on its rest. "He created lucky coins and quite a number of them, too. There are a few things people don't realize about luck and magic. There is a balance to both of them that cannot be disrupted. One should always be aware that not all luck is good."

"And magic?" Miranda asked.

"There are rules that should never be broken," Zulana explained. "There is a price to pay for everything. What the coins ended up doing was stealing good luck from anyone around their owners. At first glance, they gave their holders everything they desired. Then, over time, things began to change. Those around them; those closest to them, began suffocating in negativity."

"We should speak to this man," Jeff suggested. "Do you know how we can contact him?"

"You can't," Zulana snapped.

"You don't know where he is?" Miranda pried.

Zulana shrugged her shoulders. "Some where in New Orleans. According to folklore, he is in a state of limbo, neither alive nor dead, and unable to cross over from this world to the next until every last coin has been returned. That's why one should never show up in Knollville. They are all being beckoned back to their master."

"What happens if someone uses the coin then loses it?" Jeff asked.

Zulana's eyes widened, her brow wrinkling. "The luck would return to those it originally belonged to. The universe would correct the misalignment. Potentially, the person who owned it could be lost between this world and the next."

"Like in a coma?" Jeff asked.

"It could appear that way," Zulana answered. "Detective, if in fact, you have such a coin at the precinct, it could have negative effects on many people. It shouldn't be here in the first place. These coins need to be returned. It shouldn't, and in the long run, won't be content to remain put."

"What if it is?" Miranda asked.

"Then something is very wrong in Knollville," Zulana suggested. "The only reason for it to want to stay here is if there was a strong connection to the place where its power originated."

"The Underworld?" Miranda questioned.

"I think we'd know if the gates to Hell were located next to the diner," Jeff jested.

"Don't be so sure," Zulana replied. "Just because you can't see something, doesn't mean it isn't here."

"We'll keep that in mind. Thanks for your help." Jeff parted the beaded curtain to head to the exit.

"I look forward to our next meeting," Zulana expressed. "It won't be long."

Jeff kept his head forward all the way to the car. The engine was purring before the passenger door slammed shut.

"What do you think?" Miranda asked.

Jeff exhaled through his nose. "I don't know," he muttered. "I know we agreed to take a leap of faith with this job, but the Underworld is a bit out there."

Miranda snorted. "I know, right? Let's grab a coffee and see if we can track down another possibility. Of course, we could go to the captain. Maybe he'll send us on an all expense paid trip to New Orleans."

"Yeah, right," Jeff chuckled. "That coffee sound good, though. You buying?"

Miranda swatted his arm. "I bought lunch. I think you can handle the caffeine."

A smile shadowed his face. "What do you see when you look at the coin?"

Miranda let out a breath of air. "I only glanced at it quickly. It was a coin. I didn't think there would be a quiz on it. Maybe we should sit down and compare notes when we get back to the precinct."

"The psychic must be wearing off on you," Jeff said.

"Oh, yeah," Miranda said. "Why's that?"

"Cause you are reading my mind," Jeff replied, chuckling.

"I swear in a past life you were a comedian," Miranda snorted. "This life, however, your jokes need help."

"Don't worry," Jeff said. "I won't quit my day job... not yet, anyway."

Chapter Fifteen

Sadness was a sponge. It soaked up everything that mattered, and with a mere squeeze wrung it all back out as tears. When such misery hit, it left little room for other emotions, or anything else. To an already damaged mind it was another blow, chipping away at what sanity remained.

Seren bit her lip, hoping to hold back a waterfall of tears stinging in her eyes. Every light was on and yet darkness surrounded her. Fog filled her mind, leaving her unable to recall the walk back to the office. Somehow she'd made it there -- the coin, too. It mocked her from its resting place on the desk.

That damn coin!

It was supposed to bring her luck, not grief. Her eyes shifted to the shiny circle again. Everything had been going perfectly. Everything she wanted was right there: a promotion, a whirlwind romance, a ring on her finger. It was as if someone decided she wasn't allowed to be that happy and reached out to grab a part of it back. Perhaps it was her parents from the beyond.

The knocks on her door went unanswered. Each rap was merely background static without meaning. She heard her name, but it was drowned out by the stern voice of her father warning her about using the power of the coin. She had heeded his advice for so long and in one moment of weakness caved. Maybe that was why Mike was dead. It had been him who convinced her to release to lucky piece from the binding her mother had created for it.

Her name sounded again. Her head rose, a blank stare seeing through her assistant at the door.

"Are you okay?" Timone asked.

Seren's lips trembled. The mask of complacency she wore on a daily basis shattered, replaced by despair and shock. The dam burst, tears rolling down her face, leaving behind streaks of black from her lashes.

"That would be a no," Timone said, pulling a tissue from her sleeve. "Here."

One tissue wasn't going to make much of a difference. Still, Seren dabbed under her eyes, trying not to make her liner and mascara any worse than it already was. Whoever was responsible for testing them didn't know the meaning of waterproof.

Timone sat on the opposite side of the desk, her knees locked together in a ladylike position. "It might help to talk. I have several degrees in listening."

"He's dead," Seren mumbled.

Timone licked her lips. "Who is dead?" she questioned, scooting forward a bit -- any farther and the chair might have tipped on top of her.

Seren opened her mouth. Her breath trembled before words would form. "Mike," she said in little more than a whisper. "Mike is dead."

"Mike," Timone repeated. "As in ring-on-the-finger Mike? The one you were going to marry?"

Seren's bottom lip puffed out, stopping any further speech. Her head nodded as sobs resumed.

"How?" Timone questioned.

"He was hit by a truck crossing the road," Seren squeaked. "I got there just as they were hauling his body away."

"No!" Timone exclaimed. "You poor thing. You stay right there. I'll be back."

Seren heard her assistant's words but they didn't register. Time meant nothing. It could have been five minutes or two days later when she returned with Ms. Parker in tow.

"Timone filled me in on everything!" Ms. Parker exclaimed. "Don't you worry about a thing. You take some time off. You can't possibly work under these circumstances. There are bereavement benefits."

"I can't," Seren protested. "I just started this job, and it would leave the company short-handed."

"Don't be silly," Ms. Parker argued. "We can hire a temp to take over for a couple of weeks. In fact, there was another applicant for the job hanging about. I don't think she will turn down a few weeks of work."

"Penny," Seren muttered.

"Yes," Ms. Parker replied. "I'll call her right away. We'll start with two weeks. If you need more, you will have to call in."

"Two weeks should be fine," Seren said. "Thank you." Her lips cracked. It didn't matter how many tears soaked them, they were as dry and miserable as she was.

Chapter Sixteen

Seren took in a breath of air. Her lips puckered as she blew it back out again. A window seat wasn't ideal for a first-time flier. It was, however, all the airline had left on short notice. She glanced out the small oval window as the plane prepared for takeoff.

Flight attendants scurried about, closing overhead bins and checking seat belts. As soon as the plane started moving toward the runway, they took positions to display safety instructions in time with a video that, from the looks of it, was probably made ten years prior. Somehow, through it all, the man beside her was already asleep. If only it was that easy for her, to close her eyes and drift off into any world that didn't involve nightmares. But it wasn't. In the dark, she could feel every bump and movement the plane made.

Seren felt her forehead, wiping away tiny drops of perspiration. She was breathing, but the air seemed to lack oxygen. Her hand reached above, aiming a tiny circle toward her face, instantly rewarding her with a blast of cool air -- cold enough to calm her nerves.

She closed the blind, not wanting to see when the plane left the ground. It didn't matter, though. At the exact moment of takeoff, her back pressed against the chair, pressure building as the jet's nose pointed upward. They were in the air and rising fast. Her hands squeezed the arm rests, knuckles turning white.

Seren had spent time preparing as well as she possibly could for the flight, checking out articles online. Not much of what she read, however, helped to soothe anxiety. At least one of the tricks she learned came in handy, though. Chomping furiously on gum alleviated the pressure building in her ears.

The next four hours were spent watching how other people acted in the sky. They all appeared to be frequent fliers. Not one of them looked stressed. At one point, courage found her and the blind opened to a world of marshmallow fluff. Cloud nine was right outside, begging for her to reach out and grab a piece. That moment of contentment and serene peace was disrupted as the wing sliced through the cloud, scattering it into numerous smaller bits. A moment of turbulence followed. The lights flickered and the fasten seat belt sign flashed on.

Seren double-checked the lock on her lap; not that she had undone it at anytime during the flight. She shut the blind, refusing to watch an approaching storm, or worse, a strange monster climbing about on the wing. Leaning her head back, she took several deep breaths with her eyes closed, making the sign of a cross over her chest with one hand. Until that moment, she hadn't considered taking any religion seriously. Listening to her father's preaching seemed like a good idea from where she now sat. At the very least, it couldn't hurt.

The man beside her snorted in his sleep as they passed through another patch of turbulence. The plane shook, metal rattling. Her bone-dry mouth left her regretting her refusals of previous offers for drinks. Even if her stomach wasn't keen on the idea of drinking a soda, a cup of ice chips would have made her tongue happy. It was too late for wishful thinking. Even if there wasn't a rough flight, they were only thirty minutes away from their final destination. The landing was about to begin.

Seren considered palming the coin, but chose not to. Mike's death had shaken her faith in it, to the point she wasn't sure if it would ever completely return. That didn't mean she was foolish enough to leave it behind, though. If there was one thing she was certain of it was that, for good or for bad, her luck piece still had a role to play in her life.

Chapter Seventeen

Stepping off the plane was like entering another world. Everyone had smiles on their faces, beads around their necks, and drinks in their hands. Without leaving the airport, New Orleans was already living up to her expectations.

She stood in a line for a taxi to take her to her hotel. Technically, she was arriving early. Mardi Gras meant *Fat Tuesday* in French. It was the Friday before. Still, celebrations were well underway.

With her face practically pressed up against the glass window of the cab, Seren took in all the details she could as they whirled by. She wanted to see everything, do everything, and most of all, experience everything. This was the trip she had waited her whole life to take. This was where she would find an answer to all her questions.

The check-in process for her room went smoother than she anticipated. With crowds usually came long lineups and she was more than prepared to wait in a few. The hotel staff, however, were more than helpful. A key card was in her hand and a bracelet around her wrist in less than ten minutes.

She headed to her room to drop off the one bag she'd brought along. A quick shower and change was all she needed and she was on her way out the revolving lobby door again, flashing her wristband at the security for them to acknowledge she was a paying customer of the establishment. Technically such a gesture was only needed upon re-entry, but there was no need to take any unnecessary chances.

A blast of sticky hot air punished her for the short visit with its rival; air conditioning. Heat was one thing. Humidity, however, was worse, making the air thick and her lungs sweat. A curl sprang out of her carefully tied back hair, protesting any further outdoor ventures. She exhaled upward, blowing it off her face. There was no amount of styling products that could help, wandering about on hot pavement in the midday sun.

After taking only a few steps, she already had a hurricane in hand. The red alcohol punch went down as smooth as juice; a dangerous hazard to anyone not accustomed to alcoholic beverages. She easily could have downed three or four in a row within a two-block radius, and ended up plastered before the sun even considered going down for the day. Knowing that, she waved off an offer for a second, opting to find a bottle of cold water instead. Not an easy task with the first parade of the day making its way toward her.

She froze, unprepared for the crowd that swarmed, seeking out all the best spots. Seren waited patiently. Stories about the floats, gliding through the streets, tossing goodies into the masses swirled in her mind. Her heart fluttered as music bellowed in the background and the first vehicles came into sight.

Seren's lips curled upward in anticipation. She matched the movements of the rest of the onlookers, waving her hands high above her head. Scantly dressed women and men tossed out prizes from the floats. Her first effort to catch some failed. The next, she jumped, her fingertips barely coming in contact with some beads. They fell to the ground.

"Ow!"

No one considered how whipping things at people from moving vehicles might hurt. A rather large oversight in retrospect. Still, she decided to continue to try to collect treasures of beads, hats and small toys as each float passed by.

The crowd dissipated as quickly as it formed, leaving behind a street ankle deep in garbage. Seren hadn't even seen it happen. The surroundings changed with a bat of her eye. No one else seemed to notice or mind. People trudged along, dropping their empty cups and broken plastic necklaces on the ground where they stood -- classic tourist waste. Thousands of dollars in fliers, toys, and decorations were strewn about. It made one wonder why things were tossed off floats in the first place. If it had been the money used to buy the items in the first place that was thrown, the street would have been spotless.

A new sort of parade began its way down the road: this one wasn't followed by a crowd. In fact, it was the opposite. Tourists avoided it. A convoy of street sweepers went about cleaning up the mess for celebrations to come. Schedules were posted everywhere as to what time the parades passed by particular streets. Partygoers simply had to be at the right place at the right time to never miss a thing.

Seren took a seat at the nearest sidewalk café. After briefly glancing over the menu, a single glass of white wine was the only thing ordered. With the excitement over, for the moment, the heat was front and center in her mind again. Even her blouse was soaked. She pulled the silky material from behind in an attempt to stop it from sticking to her back.

There were only a few scattered handfuls of tourists left wandering about, checking each of the shops for the perfect souvenirs. They'd swear that the potions, herbs, and shrunken heads sold in every store were genuine magical objects. That wasn't something Seren would ever fall for. Knowing the difference between the truly spiritual and a fraud was something her mother had instilled in her from birth.

A man stopped on the sidewalk less than five feet from the café, toting a saxophone. Its black case lay open on the ground with a sign that read: *If you would like a picture please donate five dollars.* A chuckle escaped on bated breath. This man was about to perform on a street corner, wearing nothing but a loincloth attached at the sides with strings. Even his feet were bare. Her eyes glanced over his chocolate skin, the same tone her mother's had been. There was nothing else particularly notable about him. She'd seen better looking and worse. It had to be his music that people were expected to pay for.

He wet his lips, focused on his craft. The instrument lifted to his mouth. The first few notes sounded more like a warm-up than a song. Then the man's head bobbed, sporting a toothy grin. His foot tapped against the hot pavement. Music poured out, filling the road.

Seren sighed. The sound wasn't bad, but it also wasn't record label quality. Both her parents had enjoyed a good jazz set. She grew up listening to some of the best. This, in comparison, was a let-down. Still, she was curious as to how many people would pay the cover charge to stop for a picture.

A group of three women were the first to notice him. Seren eyed them up and down as they huddled in a close-knit group. Why they were giggling didn't make any sense. The music wasn't that bad it deserved ridicule. Each held up a phone and snapped a picture, dropping their offerings on the way by.

Seren turned her attention back to the man giving his all to his craft. Every note seemed to resonate through his body. Every muscle moved in time to the beat.

Her hand smacked over her mouth, covering the gaping hole that had formed. The pictures and request for cash made sense. It wasn't the privilege of listening that folks were expected to pay for. This man was noticeably well hung. The loincloth he toted barely covered his length, which was at least partially hard and bobbing up and down in time with the music. Although technically nothing was exposed, his performance left little to the imagination.

Seren's chuckle faded. Having a good time without Mike was bitter sweet. There were so many things she planned to do with him; so many places they should have been exploring together. Even in New Orleans, loss had caught up to her. It was time to move; to once more regain the lead and attempt to stay a few steps ahead of despair.

She reached in her purse, searching for money to pay for her drink. Her hand returned with a single shiny coin. Seren inhaled deeply, concentrating on the tiny circle that changed her life. Not even the music ending broke her concentration.

The musician approached her table, alternating his glance between the coin and her face. A business card landed in front of her.

"This is what you are looking for," he said before returning to his spot on the sidewalk.

Seren glanced down at the piece of stock card lying in wait. "Voodoo Treasures," she whispered. "We open at dusk."

Chapter Eighteen

Everything happened for a reason. That was something even her parents both agreed on. Using that logic, Seren was given the card for a purpose. Finding out why was at the top of her list of activities for the evening. The truth was Mardi Gras, when compared to how her parents had described it, wasn't as magical in person. Disappointment became the next emotion in line, waiting to take a shot at her gut. The only way to stop it was buried within herself. She needed to find a way to shake the feeling her experiences should have been just as amazing, if not better than, those of her parents.

There was enough time for a cold shower and a bite to eat before the sun started to settle in a fiery orange glow. That was the time to hit the sidewalk with confidence. Her strut, however, almost landed her on her backside. A frown crossed her face as one shoe slid across the slippery pavement. A bubble popped on her nose. A simple glance over a shoulder brought the smile back to her lips.

Street festivals, in any city, were a source of unhindered excitement. Here, they were the heart and soul of the land. Sidewalks were littered with tables, displaying wares from every shop. Alcohol flowed from roadside booths to anyone who could still walk and had money left in their pockets. The loud music blaring from one shop or another added to the ambiance. What wasn't expected was for a disc jockey to be set up, releasing waves of bubbles in time to his set. Anywhere else, it would have been the perfect scenario for a lawsuit. In New Orleans, it was merely another attraction.

Even without a parade, the nightlife was far more active than the afternoon had been. Tiny white lights illuminated costumes in bright colours. Feather boas and shiny baubles created rainbows around the necks of partygoers. Those without a collection flashed their bodies at anyone willing to offer them some for free.

The humidity hadn't changed much. In fact, if anything, the air seemed a bit denser. Making her way down the street, Seren chose to ignore the shops she'd peered in earlier. There was nothing that interested her in them. If she was going to do any shopping it was going to be in a legit establishment -- something off the beaten track. Hopefully, the address she'd been given would lead her to exactly that.

Two men, who couldn't have been much older than the drinking age, dragged a companion between them. The young lad's feet were already unable to work properly under the burden of a few too many hurricanes. His eyes rolled to the back of his head as he mumbled a few words no one but he would ever understand.

It was flashy. It was exciting. It was fake. There was no magic in the air. Everything around her was merely there to make money. Unfortunately, she was stuck right in the middle of it.

Normally, crowds travelled as one mass in a single direction. Each person still retained the feeling they were moving as an individual. Trying to go against the flow was completely different. This crowd, however, acted as if it were confused. People shoved and pushed, trying to reach one destination or another. No one cared about whose toes were being tread on.

Seren found herself swimming up stream against the current. Salmon at least had a good reason when they did it. The effort she was exerting was well above the norm for shopping. Her urge, however, was as great as those fish. There was no rhyme or reason to it. She simply needed to locate the store and her soul wouldn't rest until she did.

A turn off the main route left her walking in shadows. Sight, however, was the only one of her senses dulled by the side street. Music still blared and scents of alcohol mixed with various types of food wafted through the air, searching out patrons looking to enjoy exquisite seafood dishes or try a bit of gator. Apparently it tasted similar to chicken.

It was the second turn that left her completely alone. There were no streetlights, nor did any of the buildings look open. Still, her legs carried her on, determined to bring her to the satisfaction of having found what she was looking for. She chuckled, unsure how her feet knew what her brain didn't.

Since there was no sense in trying to navigate in an area where most of the streets were closed, there was also no traffic. She had the entire road to herself, which was probably a good thing -- it was only a smidge wider than an alley.

Seren came to an abrupt stop. Her gaze locked on set of open wooden doors and matching shutters, their original green colour worn from time. The rest of the building was in an equally poor state. Only parts of the brick remained visible under coats of aging plaster. Layers of bandages had been applied without first treating the wound. Sign and rope lights, dangling from an overhang, appeared to be the only additions from the present century. She held her breath. This was the place.

The store was packed to the brim with merchandise, but lacked clientele. Wooden masks and hand-sewn dolls lined the walls. Simply by sight, she could tell they weren't the brightly coloured tourist items offered in every nickel-and-dime store. A chill ran down her spine, leaving the goosebumps, only a cold breeze was previously thought to be able to produce, on her arms. She shivered, finding some of the store's offerings truly frightening.

There were other items, however, that claimed her attention as well. A huff left her lips at the sight of do-it-yourself kits for luck, love and fortune, mixed in with candles named for different rituals. These products were mass-produced and designed to make profit off of those who didn't posses a third eye. Apparently real magic wasn't where the money was -- the bills needed to be paid.

A tap on her shoulder was enough to elicit a small scream. Seren jumped backward, away from the woman glaring back at her through midnight eyes. White and black face paint formed the outline of skeleton, hiding all signs of humanity. Beneath her formal black suit with tails, female curves remained obvious. A top hat, adorned with large red plastic flowers, put a finishing touch to the over-the-top costume.

"Can I help you?" she asked, her Southern accent more than prevalent.

Seren gulped back what little saliva her dry mouth could produce. Her voice had run for the hills, leaving her behind. It returned just as quickly with gold fever, having seen a flicker of the metal around the stranger's neck.

"Your necklace," Seren croaked.

"It's a replica of a luck coin," the woman replied. "We make them ourselves."

Seren's eyes bulged. She had found someone who knew about her coin.

"You've seen one before," the woman continued.

"Yes," Seren answered. "I'm not sure how lucky it is, though. Can you tell me about it?"

"Luck is an interesting topic," the woman explained. "It's not always good. It is best to remember that. There is a delicate balance that needs to be preserved."

Seren held open her hand, displaying the circular piece of metal that had been tightly clenched within it. "Is this real? Is this an actual lucky coin?"

The woman glanced at the outstretched hand. "It may be," she answered. "What is it you are looking for?"

"Answers," Seren admitted. "At first I was happy. Then something horrible happened. I'm trying to make sense of the death of someone I love."

"The coin doesn't bring luck to those around you," the woman said. "It is the complete opposite, actually. It steals their happiness to give to you."

"But..." Seren stuttered, "I was getting married. How can I be happy when he is dead? Doesn't that go against the purpose of the coin?"

The woman paused, eyeing Seren up and down. "That is strange. Usually the effects on those closest to the bearer are less extreme. Are you sure you were both in love?"

"What kind of a question is that?" Seren barked, her nostrils flaring. Had she been a dragon, there would have been nothing left of the shop or its keeper.

"What did you come here for?" the woman questioned.

Seren paused in thought. "I need to find a way to set things right. I want to reverse what happened."

"No one can bring back the dead," the woman replied with a chuckle. "Nor would you want to."

"I have to do something!" Seren cried.

"There may be a way," the woman admitted. "You would need to be sure this is the route you want to take."

"I would do anything," Seren admitted.

"Very well." The woman placed a hand-sewn doll on the counter. "This is all I can offer, but it comes at a price."

"A voodoo doll?" Seren questioned, her forehead wrinkled with concern.

"It is a time travel doll," the woman said. "It will take you back to set things right... if that is truly what you want."

Desperation crept into Seren's eyes as she ogled the prize. "How much?"

"The coin," the woman said. "I will exchange it for the coin and only the coin."

"If it is as troublesome as you claim, why would you want it?" Seren asked.

"To send it back from whence it came," the woman replied, an eerie tone lingering in the air. "This is the only help I can offer you."

"Fine," Seren agreed. "How does the doll work?"

"Find a comfortable spot," the woman instructed, "and close your eyes. The doll in one hand and this pin in the other. Then imagine the time you want to be in and stick the doll."

"That's it?" Seren questioned.

"When you open your eyes, you will have returned to that time," the woman said. "Be forewarned, not everything may be as you hope. Going back we often see things we didn't the first time around. Those details can hold meanings we never understood before."

"Got it," Seren answered, barely listening. The doll was already in hand and the coin forgotten. She was going to save Mike and be as happy as her parents were... no matter what it took.

Chapter Nineteen

Magdella's hand caressed the wood that stood between her and destiny. Outside the heat and humidity raged out of control, reaching new records that had meteorologists scrambling to understand. Behind that door, however, was a cool dark room that was even harder to explain.

Being afraid wasn't the problem. She knew what was in the room and had come to terms with it years ago. It was the transition from one extreme to the other that was to blame for her reluctance to move.

She took in a deep breath, hoping for the best. A blast of arctic temperatures slapped her across the face. She exhaled, the air freezing in a cloud the moment it left her lips. The door slammed shut as soon as she crossed over the threshold. The hairs on her arms and neck stood up in protest of the ominous and chilled surroundings.

Her brother knelt before a fireplace, a poker in one hand and log in the other. If it were up to her, the ash would have been cleaned out on a daily basis. Her brother, however, was the expert. According to him a couple of inches of ash insulation made all the difference in keeping fires that much hotter. Heat was exactly what the room needed.

"You are back early," he said, still facing the blaze. "Why did you close the shop?"

"Another returned home," she replied. "Ricco, do you think this could be the end?"

"Let me see it," he said, extending an arm behind his back. Sparks flew up as he poked the burning logs mercilessly. "Are you sure this one is real?"

"Yes," Magdella answered, inching around the leather recliner between them. The coin dropped into his palm.

"Sit," Ricco ordered, examining the round piece he'd been given. "Let's hope this does the trick."

The couch was the most awkward piece of furniture to sit on. It wasn't always that way, though. The poor sofa had simply seen a few too many seasons. Small holes had crept in where material wore thin and a few springs prodded anyone who dared to thump down a little too hard. It had its use, though. That room only had one occupant who needed to be kept comfortable.

She eyed her brother's movements as he dragged a treasure chest into the middle of the room. The rusting remains of a lock fell to the ground; the lid creaked open.

Ricco pressed his lips against the coin. "Here goes nothing!" he exclaimed, flicking the luck piece in the air. It twirled several times before heading down to meet its siblings waiting below. With a clang, it was home.

The fire crackled laughter, flames rising to new heights in the background. A soft orange glow illuminated the treasure before them. Hundreds of coins almost completely filled the chest.

Magdella shifted her attention to the recliner. A white-haired man sat motionless, waiting. His eyes were fixed in her direction without knowing she was there. They were dead in every way, reflecting the torment his soul continued to suffer.

"Nothing happened," she muttered, a sigh hanging on her words.

"There must be more coins," her brother suggested. "Don't worry, we'll find them... or they will find us."

"I was so sure we were at the end," Magdella said. "I can't stand to see him suffer."

"He made his bed," Ricco replied. "His family has been paying for his mistakes since. It is us who suffer the most. Until every coin he gave away returns, we are in the same boat as our grandfather... none of us can rest." He returned to his duty at the hearth.

"How many more times can we do this?" she questioned. "The chest is almost full."

"I wish I knew, sister," Ricco answered. "Hopefully the next one will be the last. We'll need more wood tomorrow. I'll need you to stay while I get it."

Magdella nodded at her brother. "I'll come here before opening up for the day."

Chapter Twenty

The room key landed in front of the television; purse on the desk. Seren's eyes shifted to her own reflection. The definition of a hot mess glared back at her; a girl reminiscent of who she had been not long ago. Humidity wreaked havoc on her hair. Stray curls boldly defied the do they had been confined to, popping out in too many places to count. She released the ties and pins that bound them. A tissue removed what was left of running makeup.

Seren flopped back on the bed, allowing herself to bounce. Hotels were always much more comfortable than anything she could afford at home. One day, she'd have the money to hire a maid to make things perfect on a daily basis. Her promotion was a start in the right direction. All she was missing was Mike.

She held the doll up in front of her face. It wasn't the sort of toy a child would take to bed. The material it was made of resembled the mesh bags onions were sold in at the grocery store, with roughly stitched edges. Two odd buttons had been placed approximately where eyes should have been. Feathers and patches were attached in ways that made no apparent sense. A sigh passed through slightly parted lips. Perhaps she had been too hasty in making the trade.

She shook her head, her vision fogging. Being negative wasn't helping the situation. She needed to have confidence; she needed to believe. Her father's face appeared, disappointment dripping from his eyes. Her heart raced; nausea forcing bile up her throat. Seren grabbed the television remote and tossed it at his shaking head. He disappeared on contact.

Her eyes closed. "I am going back," she whispered. A new picture emerged in her mind; Mardi Gras, but it wasn't the one outside her hotel. It was the bar where she'd first met Mike. With the doll pressed tightly against her chest in a hug, she begged to go back -- for a chance to save Mike from a death he hadn't deserved. A pin found its way to the heart of the rag figure.

Her mind searched for the details, the grain of the wood that made the bar, the sparkle of the glasses, the booths by the window and Carl the bartender.

"Hello," Carl said, his voice rose slightly.

Seren chuckled, his voice sounded real, as if it were right beside her. The daydream was almost perfect. The only thing it lacked was Mike. Her focus intensified.

"Look, lady, I don't have all day," Carl complained. "What can I get you?"

Seren opened her eyes. Her mouthed joined in, her jaw dropping to allow a gasp to escape. Lips trembling, she huffed a single chuckle. "I'm here!" she exclaimed. "I'm really here."

She surveyed the room, looking for any confirmation it was real. Everything looked as it should. A small lunchtime rush was scattered around the room. Each party hoped they found seats far enough from anyone else to conduct private conversations with out the worry of eavesdroppers. Her lips curled upward, twitching in the corners.

Carl rolled his eyes. "Yeah. You are here. I am here. So how about you order?"

"Wait, what day is it?" Seren asked, her eyes darting back and forth.

"If you are looking for the specials..."

"Never mind," Seren interrupted. "What about Mike?"

"Mikey?" Carl's brows arched. "He isn't in yet."

Seren's phone lit up in her hands. Her mouth fell open. "He's still alive," she muttered, her lips curling up further. "I did it! I made it back!"

"What?!" Carl questioned. "Look I need you to order something or leave. I have paying customers to take care of."

"I'm waiting for Mike," Seren explained. "I'm meeting him here." She glanced out the window. Her gaze fell on a man on the opposite side of the road. She gasped; realizing simply making it back in time wasn't enough. She still needed to save him. Dropping everything on the table, she raced for the door.

"Hey!" Carl yelled.

"I'll be back," she called back. "Pour two to celebrate. Watch my things for me, too. Thanks, Carl."

Carl shook his head. A toothpick twirled in his mouth as he glanced over her belongings. A peculiar doll was the only item of interest. Phone in hand, he pressed speed dial number one.

"Hey," Carl said. "There's something here you might want to look at. Better hurry. I have a gut feeling things are about to get freaky."

Chapter Twenty-One

There was no time to think. She had made it back to a point only moments before Mike was destined to die. Stopping him from crossing the street was the only thing that occupied her mind. She raced out the door, her limbs shaking as she ran. It didn't matter how fast she begged them to move, the pavement was quicksand. Every step she took became heavier and more difficult.

The street was busy -- busier than usual. Normally, watching people scurry about would bring a grin to her face. At that moment, however, she couldn't have cared less about the businessmen with mistresses draped over their arms; addicts looking for a fix to make it through another day at a job they hated; or members of the P.T.A. hitting the sauce a little too hard before having to pick up little Jimmy and Jenny at school.

Her arms flailed, pushing anyone and everyone from her path. None of them noticed the urgency of her movements. Swear words and complaints barely registered in her ears. Even if they had, she didn't give a hoot about any of them. She wasn't about to waste the one chance she'd been given.

The sun glared directly in her eyes. She patted down her sides, but had left her purse and by extension, sunglasses in the bar. Her hand cupped, forming a poor excuse for a shield. Mike's outline was undeniable, but she couldn't make out any details.

Her vision shifted. The light was red -- the orange hand demanding all who wanted to pass stop and wait. Waiting was one thing she couldn't afford to do. There was no telling when or how the accident was going to happen. The last time she had arrived after it was over and never saw those details. Technically, all she knew was that she was in the right spot.

Seren took the first brave step, hopping off the sidewalk. Her legs took over, one foot after the other, picking up speed as they moved. Warnings became muffled noises, nothing more than background static ruining the song she was performing.

A tug on one leg stopped her in her tracks. Her heel was caught in a manhole in the middle of the road. She glanced down at it, memories of the worst day of her life flooding back.

Her head snapped back forward, her gaze meeting Mike's. He stood watching her, a question forming on his face, but no words left his lips. She searched for the meaning, but found only another woman on his arm. A woman she knew.

"Penny," Seren mumbled, her hand slapping over her mouth. She glanced down at her hand. The ring was gone.

Penny was the one who should have been hired for the promotion. Penny was the one who belonged with Mike. Penny was the person whose luck she had stolen. It all became clear now. She had made one vital mistake. She traded the coin to go back in time. She had reset her life to what it was before.

Coming back without it meant she didn't need to set things straight. She had effectively erased everything good that had happened to her.

She glanced up, seeing her own reflection in metal. The woman who stood before her wasn't a confident business woman. She was the poor excuse for life, who struggled just to make it to the next day. What did that mean? Her parents images both appeared, arms crossed over their chests... judging her as the always had.

Chapter Twenty-Two

Miranda held the cardboard tray toward Jeff. He was quick to grab a cup. There was nothing better than an afternoon infusion of caffeine to get the juices flowing. An overenthusiastic hand squeezed a bit too hard. The lid popped off, unleashing a wave of hot coffee all over his lap.

"You need to stop doing that," Miranda suggested, searching the glove box for a handful of napkins.

"They won't do much good for this spill," Jeff admitted. "I'll have to stop off at home to change."

Miranda chuckled. "As long as I've known you, this is only the second time I've seen you spill your precious java. It almost feels like dèjá vu."

"Dèjá vu," Jeff repeated, dropping the cup and the rest of its contents. "Exactly!"

"What are you doing?" Miranda screeched, grabbing the rest of her stash of paper towels. She was used to her partner's frequent messes, but this was well beyond normal, even for him. "At least try to clean it up!"

"No time," Jeff replied, one hand on the door handle. He glanced over his shoulder then back to the road in front of them.

Miranda followed his line of sight. Her eyes widened; jaw dropping. "What is going on?"

"I don't know," Jeff admitted, "but I am going to find out." His car door popped open immediately after a speeding truck. Blaring music vibrated their car with force. The truck driver wasn't about to hear a thing. If he wasn't paying attention, there was going to be a new accidental death in Knollville. This one made as little sense as the others. "Call for back up... and an ambulance!"

Miranda nodded, watching her partner go from standing still to the fastest she'd ever seen him move in a split second. The rest of her body might have been focused on calling for assistance, but her line of sight never left him and the girl he was racing to help.

The fates had already decided the outcome. It was obvious there was a zero percent chance Jeff was going to out-run the truck. With help on the way, Miranda joined in the pursuit.

"Get off the road," Jeff yelled up ahead, his arms flailing.

The woman, whoever she was, wasn't listening. She stood, the likes of a deer caught in headlights, except she wasn't facing her impending doom. Truth be told, it appeared she had no idea a truck was about to plow her over. The woman's attention was focused on something or someone in front of her on the side of the road.

Jeff came to a complete stop. It was too late. He spun around, teeth grinding and eyes clenched. A blaring horn and thud signalled it was all over. A moment for composure was all he needed before he was back on track. This time not to stop a death, but to investigate one.

The truck rolled to a screeching halt. The driver hopped out, his body shaking. "She was in the middle of the road. The light was green," he stuttered.

"Didn't you see her?" Jeff questioned, walking past. There was no need to rush now. Even from yards out he knew the woman died on impact. "I saw her a couple of blocks away. Don't go anywhere."

Jeff knelt down on the road, pulling a pair of gloves from a pocket. Even if death was a forgone conclusion, it was procedure to check for any signs of life. He shook his head, surveying the rest of the scene. The woman's pulse wasn't the only thing she was missing.

"Find anything?" Miranda asked.

"Nothing," Jeff admitted. "No purse, no phone, and no identification. Why was she in the road?" He ignored his partner for the moment. The question wasn't for her. It was for himself.

"There's a crowd forming," Miranda said.

"See if you can hold them off until backup arrives," Jeff mumbled. "And keep witnesses separated from newcomers. I want to know what happened here."

"I know that look," Miranda said.

"Yeah," Jeff replied, "but this time you saw for yourself something wasn't right."

"I thought the string on non-accidental accidents ended with Truly, though," Miranda whispered.

"Not even you could think this was a coincidence," Jeff said, his voice stern. "Something stopped her in her tracks and I want to know what. The only way that is going to happen is if someone else saw it too."

Miranda glanced around all sides of the street. Knowing where to start was a problem. The woman had to have come from somewhere. Her handy notepad flipped open, ready for another round of who-done-it clues. Each establishment surrounding them was given its own page. That didn't nail down the moments prior to the victim's death, though. She closed her eyes, remembering the scene before the truck plowed through the woman. A much nicer setting than the blood and guts now decorating the asphalt.

Her eyes blinked open, glaring in the direction the victim must have been coming from. A smile twitched at the sides of her mouth, not forming fully out of respect for the deceased. There was only one place that made sense: Mardi Gras Bar & Grill.

The tavern door opened, a man stepping out. He looked both ways on the sidewalk, completely ignoring the accident site and other gawkers. Pulling up his jacket collar, he ducked out of sight, down an alley.

Miranda froze; luckily instinct had already kicked in. There were a couple of pictures waiting for future examination on her phone if she needed them. Under normal circumstances she would have followed a suspicious suspect herself. This particular person, however, she knew how to find without stalking. What didn't make sense was what her predecessor was doing there and why he didn't come to help them. Henry might have been in the process of retiring, but he had to have known a woman died. Wasn't he still bound to his duty to lend aid to the public or his fellow officers?

"Everything okay?" Jeff asked.

"Yeah," Miranda answered. "I'm going to send our witnesses into the bar to wait. I have a feeling that's where we are going to find a lot of our answers."

Chapter Twenty-Three

Jeff left the scene in the capable hands of another team of officers. They were already questioning the truck driver. While he should have been paying better attention, it was unlikely he could have avoided hitting someone determined to take their own life. There was nothing outside that was going to help solve the riddle surrounding this death: not the driver and not the body. The latter was mangled beyond identification purposes. That left the people crowded into the bar. He shook his head. This was probably the most business that joint had in years. That in itself could have been a motive.

It took Jeff a minute to locate his partner from the door. The booth she had chosen was slightly hidden from his view.

"Hi," he said, sliding in beside her.

"This is my partner, Jeff," Miranda said, her nose stuck between the pages of her notebook. She turned to her partner. "This is Mike and his girlfriend, Penny. They are regulars here and were about to cross the street when the accident happened."

"Can I fetch you anything?" Carl asked.

Jeff flashed his badge. "Can you stay for a moment? We have a few questions."

"Sure," Carl said, wiping his hands on a once-white apron. "I'm not sure how I can help, though."

"Did any of you know the deceased?" Miranda questioned.

"She came in here a few times," Carl answered. "I keep my distance from most of the patrons. She was an odd ball."

"That's putting it mildly," Mike blurted out, rolling his eyes, earning him an elbow from his girlfriend.

"Be nice," Penny ordered. "She is dead, after all."

"Odd in what way?" Jeff asked, ignoring the blonde. "Was it something she did or said?"

"Just odd," Mike replied. "From the first time I saw her, I sensed something was off."

"I remember that," Carl agreed. "She showed up during a bad storm. She was soaked through and through; her knees all scraped up."

"And ranting and raving about how bad her day was," Mike added. "Then she had no money."

"Except that weird coin," Carl said.

"Coin?" Jeff questioned. "What coin?"

"She said it was a good luck piece," Mike replied. "It was in a strange box."

"And she didn't want to open it," Carl blurted out. "She said her parents told her the lucky piece was evil or something. I wasn't actually paying that much attention. I figured she was a con artist or a moocher. Either way, I didn't want her sticking around too long."

"But you let her stay?" Miranda inquired.

"Mikey paid for a drink," Carl scoffed.

"I felt bad for her," Mike complained. "Honestly, I thought she was going to commit suicide right then and there."

"She didn't, though," Jeff said.

"Nah," Mike replied. "She passed around the box, showing off that coin like it was her religion... kept talking about her parents, too."

"Then what?" Miranda asked.

"I don't remember seeing her again until today," Mike answered.

"Come to think of it," Carl added, "I don't either. She was sitting at a booth and I was trying to take her order. She was acting all weird, asking what the date was. Then she wanted to know where Mike was and ran out, leaving all her things behind."

"She was asking about me?!" Mike exclaimed. "Why would she do that?"

"Good question," Penny mumbled.

"We'll need those things," Miranda stated. "What about you? Did you know the deceased?"

"Not really," Penny said. "She used to work for the same firm as me, but I never spoke to her. She was fired the day I was hired. There was a lot of office gossip about it."

"Here's her purse and coat," Carl said, returning from behind the bar. "I didn't touch anything, other than to move it aside when the place started filling up."

Jeff opened the purse and noted the contents. "Is this the box?" he asked, placing a small wooden container on the table.

"Yeah," Mike replied. "That's it."

"It's empty," Jeff commented, exchanging glances with his partner. "No sign of the coin in her purse."

"Nothing in her pockets, either," Miranda said.

"What does a coin have to do with her death?" Mike asked. "Everyone saw what happened. It was an accident."

"Or suicide," Miranda suggested. "We need to cover all bases for our report. Plus, her next of kin might be looking for the coin. Especially if it was as important to the deceased as you say."

"Of course," Penny agreed, patting her boyfriend's arm. "You'll have to excuse us. We were on our way here to celebrate our engagement. I think we are still in shock."

"Congratulations," Miranda replied. "I'm sorry the circumstances aren't better for your celebrations."

"Would you recognize the coin if you saw it?" Jeff asked, moving the niceties to the side.

"Yeah," Carl admitted. "She showed it off like it was her newborn baby, and it wasn't exactly good looking... if you know what I mean."

Jeff pulled up a picture on his phone of the coin from his previous case. "Is this it?"

Carl and Mike both moved in close to view all the different angles available.

"Yeah, that's it," Carl admitted, scratching his head. "Did you find it outside?"

"I can't reveal those details," Jeff replied, tucking his phone back into his interior suit pocket.

"Details," Mike echoed. "Is this an investigation?"

"No," Miranda replied, jumping into the conversation to smooth things over. Jeff had a knack of upsetting people to the point of complaints being filed. "We simply cannot discuss details of any death with anyone before next of kin has been notified. I'm sure you understand."

Mike nodded. "Yeah, sure." He side-eyed Jeff, keeping him in view. "Do you need anything else?"

"No," Miranda answered. "Not at the moment. I have your contact information. If anything comes up, we'll give you a call." She nudged her partner to leave the booth.

"Sergeant," Jeff called, moving toward the door. "Can you finish taking names and addresses?"

"Sure thing," the man answered.

"Thanks," Miranda added, following her partner out the door. She tugged on his arm. "You think there is a connection between the coins, don't you?"

"I do," Jeff admitted. "Why else would they look the same? Even you must find that too big a coincidence to overlook."

"Yeah," Miranda agreed, frown lines forming between her brows. "It is. I think we should head back to the office."

"Why's that?" Jeff questioned.

"Because there is someone there who might have a few of the answers," she suggested.

"And who might that be?" Jeff asked.

"Henry," Miranda replied. "I saw him leaving the bar earlier. He was trying to hide in plain sight."

"He was here and didn't offer a hand?" Jeff questioned. "That doesn't seem like something Henry would do."

"I know," Miranda agreed. "If I hadn't seen him duck down an alley with my own two eyes, I would be a bit skeptical, too. But I did and I have the photos to prove it." She held up her phone, waving it back and forth.

"I wonder how he fits into all this," Jeff muttered.

"I don't know, but this isn't the way I'd expect a semi-retired officer to act. Hopefully we don't have a problem with the captain's friend."

Chapter Twenty-Four

He had said it before and he would say it again, Henry Doogalen wasn't a stereotypical officer. He never wore a uniform; instead the man dressed in plain clothes. Of course, even that had a signature to it; one Jeff and his partner recognized every time they met the man.

Henry always waltzed in; unzipped his windbreaker jacket and hung it off the back of a chair or hook. A flat grey cap would be placed down on any surface in front of him before he himself would take a seat.

Jeff's trip down memory lane reminded him of evidence of years of dedication to the force etched into Henry's face. They weren't normal scars, but each and every wrinkle had its own story to tell, if one wanted to listen.

Once ginger hair was now streaked with grey, matching a bushy moustache. That alone wasn't an indicator of age, though, but rather a testament to the man's strength in overcoming adversities. They were the signs proving he had faced and bested more than his fair share of those in his lifetime. Henry Doogalen's physique, however, gave away his age. No amount of lifting or exercise stopped the effects of time. There was little doubt he was past the retirement age. Still, he stuck around, offering tidbits of information here and there when requested. Now the question was raised; was he helping or hindering investigations?

Jeff rolled his chair from one desk to another. That was the best part of having an entire office with only two detectives. The space let him spread out to wherever he chose, without cluttering his own work space.

The first station offered a view of the crime scene from the park. Truly's life was now a dream world, locked in a coma she'd never awaken from. She had been the victim of a theft. The robber fared even worse, ending up face down in a pile of wet cement. Pictures of the coin found by his body littered the desk. That was the connection between the two cases, but what did it mean?

He swivelled in another direction to glance over the notes from their visit with the psychic. If he believed her, an evil game was afoot in Knollville. Unfortunately, he wasn't sure he believed her, or any of the so-called paranormal proof he'd been shown. The only thing he agreed to, in taking his current position, was to keep an open mind. That didn't mean he was going to forgo logical thought. So far, everything he'd come across had a possible answer that didn't fall into the supernatural realm as well as one that did. Neither side could be proven or disproved, for that matter.

The final desk had pictures of the accident scene from earlier that day. A file folder still contained the gruesome details of the deceased's body. There was no need to look at the goriest aspects. The rest of the pictures were print outs from Miranda's phone.

Jeff held a magnifying glass to the first one. The man in question was without doubt Henry. What he was carrying, however, proved much more difficult to make out.

He cupped his chin between thumb and forefinger, focusing on the image.

"Find something interesting?" Miranda asked, depositing a tray holding coffee cups on her desk. She pulled her sweater off, letting it fall in a clump on her chair.

"Hey," Jeff said without averting his attention. "You didn't happen to notice what Henry was carrying when he left the bar, did you?"

Miranda took the picture from him, pulling it close to her face. Her teeth grazed her bottom lip.

"I'll take that as a no," Jeff said, snapping the photograph back. "Squinting doesn't make things bigger. You need reading glasses. Make an appointment before you go completely blind."

Miranda huffed, flipping hair over her shoulder. She wasn't old enough to consider needing granny glasses yet. "Sorry," she pouted. "I was more focused on the man than what was in his arms."

"You are detective," Jeff argued. "You should have taken stock of both."

"You are a detective and you didn't see either," Miranda complained. "At least I took the pictures." Her arms crossed over her chest. "I hate it when you go into full investigator mode. You can turn into a real prick."

Jeff chuckled. "Yeah," he agreed. "I'm a jerk and plan to stay that way until we figure out exactly what is going on. I don't like being left in the dark. That's my nature. I would have thought by now you'd be used to it."

"I don't think I'll ever get used to it," Miranda complained. "And if you ask me, it isn't this case that put you in asshole mode. Everything always stems back to Truly."

"I didn't ask you," Jeff argued.

"You need to let it go," Miranda continued. "Or one day you'll end up just like her."

"In a coma?" Jeff snickered.

"Alone!" Miranda yelled. "And if you hit the wrong buttons in a coma, too." A smile formed in the corners of her lips.

Jeff laughed. "You gonna put me there?" he asked.

"Don't tell me I'm the only one close enough to you to get annoyed," Miranda joked. "I am serious about ending up alone. No one likes being belittled."

"Sorry," Jeff offered, running a hand through his hair. "I am a bit frustrated."

"I couldn't tell," Miranda said, chuckling. "Hopefully Henry can shed some light on things." She passed a coffee.

"Thanks," Jeff said, holding his cup up in an air cheers. "Did you get in touch with him?"

"Yeah," Miranda answered. "He's on his way in. You know maybe cutting down on caffeine might help your disposition. You could switch to decaf."

Jeff wagged a finger in her direction. "You are playing with fire. No one touches my caffeine!" He swallowed back a mouthful of java. "If anything, I was thinking of going to espresso."

"We could get you a room next to Truly and have them feed you coffee intravenously," Miranda jested, a full smile gracing her face.

"Now that sounds like a plan," Jeff replied. "Except then you would have to handle all the supernatural cases in Knollville alone. Who would save the precious kitties then?"

Chapter Twenty-Five

Miranda glanced at the door. From her desk she could hear the undeniable noises of the elevator doors opening and closing. It was only a moment later that Henry Doogalen strolled in.

Before saying a word, he unzipped his windbreaker and hung it on a hook attached to the wall. His cap landed on an empty desk, a small briefcase beside it.

"You two wanted to see me?" he said, taking a seat and leaning back.

"Henry," Jeff said. "It's good of you to come in so quickly. We'll try not to take up too much of your time."

Henry chuckled. "Time I have to spare," he replied. "Retirement is a tad more boring than I anticipated."

"Apparently," Jeff blurted out.

"Is something wrong?" Henry asked, alternating glances between the two detectives.

"You were seen today at an accident site," Miranda stated. "You left without offering a hand."

"Technically," Jeff added, "you aren't officially retired yet. Do you mind telling us what you were doing there?"

"And where you took off to so fast?" Miranda questioned.

"Ah," Henry said, pursing his lips. "I don't usually get involved in the normal cases."

"And you didn't happen to notice who the first responding officers were?" Miranda asked.

"No," Henry admitted. "Should I have? What does any of this have to do with paranormal cases?"

"That is exactly the question we had for you," Jeff stated, tossing a picture on the desk. "That's you exiting the bar. What did you take?"

Henry glanced down at the photograph. His hand rubbed over his chin, pulling at a few whiskers, before dropping down defeated by the question. "I was collecting a rare object," he admitted. "All good detectives have contacts. Carl happens to be one of mine."

"The bartender," Miranda commented.

"Yeah," Henry agreed. "He called me about a woman who had gone off the deep end. She left an unusual item behind he thought I should take a gander at."

"A coin," Jeff said.

Henry's brow wrinkled. "Coin? I didn't see any coin. I retrieved this." The briefcase snapped open. He offered the doll for examination.

"What is it?" Miranda questioned.

"A voodoo doll," Henry replied. "It's authentic... made in New Orleans, but I haven't been able to identify by who."

"New Orleans!" Miranda shrieked. She darted a glare at her partner. "Do you know what it does?"

"Not yet," Henry admitted. "I'm still researching it. I thought I'd pop it into the vault here to keep it out of the hands of the general public. Until we do know its capabilities it's best that way."

"You are sure you didn't see a coin," Jeff said. "It's still missing."

"Wait," Miranda complained, "we have a vault? Why didn't someone tell me before? What's in it?"

"It's where I stored all the artifacts and strange items from cases over the years," Henry replied. "The captain has the only key. I asked him to meet me down here to deposit it."

"And it was good timing," Captain Miller said from the door. "I was coming down for a chat with these two anyway."

"About what?" Jeff asked. "If it is about the cat in the tree, I still think taxpayer funds are better spent with me elsewhere."

"It's not about the cat," the captain admitted. "It's about the girl who died today. I don't know why you were there, but I thought you might want to hear the outcome."

"That was a fluke," Miranda said. "We were on the street when it happened."

"Well, it has been ruled a suicide," Captain Miller stated. "A couple of officers went to inform the next of kin and found her parents dead in their house. Seems she murdered them, left a note she was sorry, and in the end couldn't live with what she did. There were newspaper clippings in her apartment about the accidents from the Truly case. Everyone who has been interviewed agrees she was certifiable. It's a closed case."

"In other words..." Miranda started.

"Leave it alone," the captain ordered. "This one isn't worth wasting your time on. There are stacks of other cases for you to look into and plenty of cats to save."

"Fair enough," Henry replied. "Since we are all here I'd like to ask to stay on a day or two a week. I can help keep things in the department that belong here." He flashed a toothy grin.

Captain Miller nodded, a stern glare offered to each of his detectives. "All right," he agreed. "But the three of you stay out of trouble."

Henry's arm extended with the reflexes of a twenty-year-old, easily catching the keys lobbed in his direction.

"You can keep those for now," the captain said. "The less I need to come down here, the better. I don't want to raise any suspicions among the other men."

"I'll keep them safe," Henry said. "The keys and the youngins." A grin encompassed his face, the twinkle returning to his eyes.

Chapter Twenty-Six

The vault was nothing more than a walk-in closet, with a door handle lock that could have been bought at any general hardware store. Even less impressive were the items it held. Jeff glanced over the collection of dolls. The one brought back from the bar was merely the latest in a long line that spanned several decades and types.

"All of this has a supernatural connection?" Jeff questioned, keeping his hands interlocked behind his back to avoid touching anything. Just because he wasn't sure he believed in all of it, didn't mean he was willing to take any chances.

Henry placed the voodoo doll on a shelf next to the other cloth style toys. "Better safe than sorry," Henry replied. "Unfortunately we don't have any proper way to dispose of this stuff. That's why I started this room."

"And you are positive that doll belonged to the victim of today's accident," Miranda inquired.

"It did," Henry said, nodding. "We aren't investigating that, though."

"Nope," Jeff agreed. "We are merely following another lead from a different case and the two cross paths."

"The coin?" Henry asked.

"Are there any in here?" Jeff replied with questions of his own. "Have you heard of any magic coins in Knollville before?"

"No," Henry admitted, "but that doesn't mean they don't exist. What is the story behind the one you are investigating?"

"It belonged to Truly," Jeff blurted out.

"Truly?!" Henry exclaimed. "I didn't think I'd be hearing her name again."

"We pieced together that the coin found by the robber's body was hers," Miranda explained. "Witnesses identified the coin as similar to one today's victim had. We found the box she carried it in, but not the coin itself."

"That's a weak connection," Henry suggested. "Coins could appear the same to the human eye."

"Yes, I thought about that," Jeff admitted.

"But..."

"But," Jeff continued, "we have our own informant; a psychic. She identified the coin as part of a rare set -- coins that she claims have been trying to return to their original owner... in New Orleans."

"Now, that is interesting," Henry said. "I wonder how the doll fits in to all of this."

"Short of visiting New Orleans, we might never know," Miranda suggested. "There was more to worry about than the coin itself, though."

"How so?" Henry asked.

"The psychic considered it an omen that two coins had showed up in Knollville," Jeff replied. "She thought there might be more to the history of the area than we were aware of. Maybe you can fill in some blanks."

"I don't know too much more than you two do," Henry admitted. "Although, I think I might know a place to start. Let me do some research and get back to you."

"Don't take too long," Jeff jested. "It almost sounded as if we might be facing an apocalypse." His joke didn't go over well with the present crowd.

"With what I've seen over the years," Henry replied, "it wouldn't surprise me." He slapped his hat on his head and tossed his jacket over his shoulder. Waving with one hand over his head, he headed for the elevator. "I'll be in next week. Be prepared for an adventure."

Miranda shook her head. "What are we getting into? Are you ready to dive in head first?"

Jeff winked. "I don't know," he admitted. "I'll reserve my judgement until after I see what Doogalen comes up with. Until then, I'm still a skeptical paranormal investigator." He chuckled. "A hypocrite through and through."

"You know that's not a good thing, don't you?" Miranda questioned, tilting her head to wait for an answer.

"In this case, I'm not sure that's true," Jeff argued. "I think we need to question everything. That's the only way we'll know we are getting the right answers."

"I might agree with that," Miranda said.

"You agree with me?" Jeff howled a laugh. "That's gotta be a first."

"Let's hope it's not the last," Miranda said. "Come on. It's time to call it a day."

"You got coffee in the morning?" Jeff asked, turning out the lights behind them.

"Don't I always?" Miranda answered.

"Yeah I guess you do," Jeff replied. He motioned for her to enter the elevator first.

Jeff side-eyed his partner. There was a long road ahead and he wasn't sure where it was leading them, but as long as Miranda was coming along, he was content to go the distance. He still had his reservations about everyone else, though. There would most certainly be a watchful eye kept on both Henry and their psychic from there on out.

"See you tomorrow," Miranda said, heading to her car.

"Yeah," Jeff muttered. "Do me a favour? Lock your doors tonight."

"Sure," Miranda agreed, the lines on her face deepening. "Is there something I should know about?"

"Nah," Jeff said, a grin forming on his lips. "Just another gut feeling. Like Henry said... better safe than sorry. Have a good night. Tomorrow you get all the tree climbing."

The End.

Author's Message

I hope you enjoyed reading *Serendipity's Debt* as much as I did writing it.

There is much more to come from our detectives in the Welcome to Knollville Series. I hope you'll pick up the next installment, coming soon.

Until next time... happy reading!

ABOUT THE AUTHOR

C.A. King is the recipient of several awards, including: The Hamilton Spectator Readers' Choice Award for 2017 & 2018 Best Author; The Brant News Readers' Choice Award for 2017 Best Author; Readers' Favorite award in the short story/novella category; the 2017 SIBA Award for Best New Adult; the 2017 SIBA Award for Best Novella; 2018 Readers' Favorite International Book Awards: Gold Medal in the Fiction - Supernatural genre; and 2018 Readers' Favorite International Book Awards: Bronze Medal in the Fiction - New Adult genre

Currently residing in Brantford, Ontario Canada, she lives with her two sons. She began her writing career after the tragic loss of her parents and husband. Redirecting her emotions through writing became therapeutic in her battle with depression and in 2014 she decided to publish some of her works.

Other Titles from C.A. King

The Portal Prophecies

These great titles in C.A. King's The Portal Prophecies series are available now at most online book retailers:

A Keeper's Destiny

A Halloween's Curse

Frost Bitten

Sleeping Sands

Deadly Perceptions

Finding Balance

Volume I (Books 1-3)

Volume II (Books 4-6)

The prophecies are the key to their survival. Can they solve them in time?

Shattering the Effects of Time

Join the Shinning brothers, Jessie, Dezi and Pete as they set out on a quest to save their younger sister. No magic known to them or their friends has ever been able to reverse the grip of time. A few legends, however, exist mentioning ancient items that may hold the key to do exactly that.

This brand new series will take you on a search for the Fountain of Youth and Mermaids; a quest for the Holy Grail; a trip to visit Daryl the mountain guru, in the hunt for the Cinamani Stone; on a search for Ambrosia, the food of the Gods; and other adventures.

Surviving the Sins: Answering the Call

The prophecies are being rewritten. This time someone is using the seven deadly sins: Lust; Gluttony; Greed; Sloth; Wrath; Envy; and Pride, to unlock an ancient evil. The book falls into Jade's hands to answer destiny's call. Can she survive the sins?

Surviving the Sins: Pride

No one is safe when a witch's pride is at stake.

Prudance is back in Pewterclaw, and she isn't about to give up her prestigious status without a fight -- especially not because of vampires. As an eighth-generation witch, she plans to do whatever it takes to stop the proposed new legislation from becoming law, including waking the dead for help.

Humility isn't in her vocabulary. With an ego spinning out of control and ancestral power at her fingertips, Prudance weaves a plot to keep Jade and Gavin separated. Will it be enough to satisfy the spirits she summoned?

When her pride costs more than she bargained for, someone has to pay the tab -- but who will it be?

Surviving the Sins: Lust

What Mother doesn't know won't hurt her.

Lucinda has spent her entire existence running The Organization and looking after Mother's needs without complaint. That's about to change. A burning desire had manifested inside her -- one she could no longer deny... Lust.

When Constable Safron Black shows up unexpected with news of an imprisoned God, Lucinda unravels. With power fuelling her passion, she'll do anything to make Morynx her mate.

****

Jade and her friends find themselves at a standstill. They have already failed to stop Pride from completing its task and they haven't located any victims for the other six sins. A strange fire in the municipal office puts them hot on the trail of what could be answers. Will they be in time to stop the dial from moving and further opening the way for Morynx?

Gluttony

Zoe never claimed to be the virtuous type; her lack of patience was proof of that. The transition from princess to barmaid never sat well with her. Without a wand, however, there was little she could do to change things.

In one fleeting moment, her universe was turned upside down. The answer to all her problems was staring her in the face from within her brother's grasp. With control of one tiny vial, she would have her cake and everyone else's too. Turning her back on family was a small price to pay in comparison.

Joseph mentioned once that being a glutton didn't suit her. With an abundance of newfound power, she intended to prove him wrong.

When Leaves Fall: A Different Point of View Story

Ralph wakes up to what others only experience in a nightmare. Chained to a shed, he has no idea where he is, or who his captor is. His memories a blurred at best. As the days press on he finds himself experiencing a roller coaster of feelings. Hunger, thirst and pain become his only companions. Flashbacks of a happier time are all he has to keep him going. As his situation deteriorates, he finds himself doubting the very things he wants most -- a family.

When Leaves Fall is a dramatic-thriller with a twist. Keep the tissue box close for the ending.

Tomoiya's Story

A Vampire Tale. She had a secret but she wasn't the only one who had something to hide.

Book I ~ Escape to Darkness

Book II ~ Collecting Tears

Book III~ Coming Soon

Peach Coloured Daisies:

A Cursed by the Gods Story

He couldn't die. An ancient curse meant she always did. This time, that was going to change -- one way or another.

When Daisy's grandmother, her last living relative, passes away, she doesn't know where to turn. Things go from bad to worse when a local psychic tells her about a curse. Alone and confused, she ends up in front of her college professor's office, ready to cry her heart out in his arms.

Matt Demi might be the son of a God, but he's living the life of a cursed man. He's had to watch the woman he loves die on her twenty-first birthday countless times. Nothing he does seems to be able to affect the outcome. When she shows up at his office scared out of her wits by a psychic's prediction, he vows this time will be different.

With only three days, Matt will need to embrace a side of him he swore off long ago to save her, but will he lose himself in the process?

Flower Shields: A Four Horsemen Novel

Meet the four horsemen: Michael, Gabrielle, Uriel and Raphael. For centuries their job has been to guard the gates of hell, making sure they never open. Without the keys, there was never any real threat. That's about to change. There are rumours on the horizon that demon followers unearthed scrolls that explain exactly how to find the lost keys. This new battle is a race to see which side locates them first.

Michael couldn't care less about the love story behind how and why the world was created. In fact, nothing matters to him other than keeping the gates to hell closed. If one of the lost keys ever fell into the wrong hands, all humanity would be doomed. He's not going to let that happen -- at any cost.

****

Tara's life is nothing short of a disaster. She's managed to flunk out of college with about the same amount of dignity as every relationship she's been in. The only constant in her life has been her love for flowers. When she's attacked at work, a stranger comes to her aid. Michael might be good-looking, but he's also arrogant, bossy and crazy. He's also her only chance to figure out who attacked her and why. Should she follow her heart and trust him -- or listen to her head and run?

Drawing Strength From Words: A Four Horsemen Novel

Meet the four horsemen: Michael, Gabrielle, Uriel and Raphael.

For centuries their sole purpose has been guarding the sealed gates to hell. Without keys, there was never any real threat. That was about to change...

For Gabrielle, protecting mankind was merely a job for which she received little credit. The vast insecurities of men altered history itself, portraying her as a masculine brute. Taking a back seat to her brothers seemed the right thing to do, but left a bitter taste in her mouth and an impenetrable barricade shielding her heart.

****

Ryder bounced around the system from the moment both his parents were killed. Between that and run-ins with the law for crimes he never committed, it seemed the whole world was conspiring against him. Never growing attached to anyone was rule number one: a rule he'd never broken until a white-haired vixen, with blocks of ice on her shoulders, walked right into his life. Melting through those frosty layers became all that mattered, even if that meant sacrificing himself in the process.

Miracles Not Included

A heartfelt romantic story about: life; love; loss; and learning to love again. If only life came with instructions and a warning label ~ Miracles Not Included.

****

Chris was born to be a writer. Even the smallest of details couldn't pass without notice, often becoming part of a plot for her next novel. The one thing she never saw coming was her husband's sudden illness.

Jason loved his wife from the moment they met. Nothing could ever change that -- nothing except the death sentence he'd been handed -- a terminal cancer diagnosis.

His story was ending: Hers was starting a new chapter and more than one miracle was needed to turn the page.

Twisted Tales of a Dead End Street

A paranormal mystery laced with comedic undertones: Twisted Tales of a Dead End Street.

Nine neighbours were invited to the mysterious dinner party at 9 Nine Street. Their host, the owner of the mansion, had more planned for the evening than just roast beef.

When the secret of their quiet street was revealed, everything changed, blurring the lines between the tangible and the paranormal.

Was the number nine the difference between life and death? Would any of them survive long enough to uncover the truth? They would each soon find out this wasn't a simple case of who-done-it so much as one of what was being done and by whom.

Shot Through The Heart: A Faerie Tale

A tale of two worlds -- one filled with magic; the other void of it. But what happened to those trapped between the two? Adelia was about to find out...

Magic and structure were the foundations of her existence. Temptation controlled the ability to destroy everything she knew. The world of men held a powerful allure over her heart, waking that which had long been dormant. It enticed her, snagging her in a web of emotions.

A decision had to be made. Was feeling love for the first time worth sacrificing magic and immortality?

Do Not Open Until Halloween

When eighteen year old Caitlin agreed to babysit her eccentric Aunt's two cats and house, she had no idea that Justin was finally going to ask her for a date the same weekend. Torn between family and crush, she chose to take her best friends' suggestion to heart, arranging a small Friday night gathering.

Little did she know a fairy was about to crash the party with trouble hot on her wings.

Caitlin will have to dig deep to find even a smidgen of belief in magic or there won't be any hope of saving her new friend from being hunted.

In this young adult fantasy, award-winning author, C.A. King, explores the answer to one of the questions readers have always wanted to ask...

Where do fairies come from?

Truly Unfortunate

Growing up in Knoll County wasn't easy, especially without any childhood memories. Truly spent her whole life searching for the answers her mind refused to reveal. There might have been horrors in her past, but her current existence wasn't much better than a nightmare. After beginning treatments with a new doctor, disturbing visions began to resurface. The stench of death surrounded her, but where exactly was it coming from?

Jeff always knew he wanted to be one of Knoll County's finest and had no problem achieving that dream. A part of his ambition stemmed from the death of a classmate at the tender age of nine. It might have been ruled an accident, but his gut told him otherwise. When people start turning up dead in the same pattern, Jeff will be forced to put everything on the line to connect the dots between past and present. But in doing so, will his own future be jeopardized?

Truly Unfortunate is a dark paranormal thriller that will leave readers with chills after answering the question: Which is stronger... the boundaries of reality or the safety on one's own mind?

Merry Apocalypse

For centuries, families gathered throughout the holiday season to hear recitals of the famous words of Dr. Clement C. Moore's 'Twas the Night Before Christmas and celebrate the long awaited return of Santa. His jovial generosity became synonymous with all that was Merry and bright. Then everything changed.

This year, the gatherings are sharing their own Christmas story. Merry Apocalypse includes the telling of a new traditional tale that echoes the tone and rhythm of familiar poetry, but instead of joy and bliss, contains warnings of danger and death.

Sometimes Love Stinks

What's in a name? Everything when it's laughable.

Gastrella M. Balance was living a never-ending nightmare. For several years, she'd been the butt of jokes about... her butt. Moving to Knollville was a chance for a fresh start. It was a place where no one knew her past, or her name and she was determined to keep both a secret. Her strategy was to stay under the radar and as inconspicuous as possible. That plan, however, went south the first time she laid eyes on Tanner. When he noticed her, too, she couldn't help but hope for a bit of romance, no matter how far fetched it seemed.

*****

Tanner had everything a guy could ask for in his senior year of high school. He had a football in one hand and a pretty girl hanging off the other arm. Being popular and the center of attention came naturally to him. Taking tests, however, did not and he was desperate to keep that part of his life to himself.

When a series of pranks go awry, they'll both be faced with confronting their personal anxieties. Together, they might have a chance to overcome the odds and survive the year.

Sometimes Love Stinks is a romantic comedy that deals with issues that are both real and difficult. While the main characters in this story are from the mundane world, readers can expect to find the signature supernatural kiss C.A. King adds to all her books.

www.ingramcontent.com/pod-product-compliance
Lightning Source LLC
Chambersburg PA
CBHW031111260626
47172CB00001B/311